WILD THINGS

WRITTEN & ILLUSTRATED BY

clay carmichael

BOYDS MILLS PRESS
A HIGHLIGHTS COMPANY
Honesdale, Pennsylvania

For information about permission to reproduce selections from this book,
please contact permissions@highlights.com.

Library of Congress Cataloging-in-Publication Data
Carmichael, Clay.
Wild things / Clay Carmichael. — 1st ed.
p. cm.
Summary: Stubborn, self-reliant eleven-year-old Zoë, recently orphaned, moves to the country
to live with her prickly half-uncle, a famous doctor and sculptor, and together they learn about
trust and the strength of family.
ISBN: 978-1-59078-627-7 (hc) • ISBN: 978-1-59078-914-8 (pb)
[1. Family life—Fiction. 2. Self-reliance—Fiction. 3. Trust—Fiction. 4. Orphans—Fiction.
5. Uncles—Fiction. 6. Sculptors—Fiction. 7. Cats—Fiction. 8. Human-animal relationships—
Fiction.] I. Title.
PZ7.C21725Wil 2009
[Fic]—dc22
2007049911

This book includes an excerpt from
The Boy Who Drew Cats, a Library of Congress facsimile produced in 1987
through the Daniel J. and Ruth F. Boorstin Publications Fund.

10 9 8 7 6 5 4 3 2 1

BOYDS MILLS PRESS, INC.
815 Church Street
Honesdale, Pennsylvania 18431

With love to Mike, who graciously lent Henry his winged heart,
and to Mr. C'mere, wild thing and best cat ever

Love is a religion with a fallible god.
—*Jorge Luis Borges*, "The Meeting in a Dream"

Baby, we can choose you know,
We ain't no amoebas.
—*John Hiatt*, "Thing Called Love"

Humans were diggers and buriers, the cat thought, like dogs.

The day the girl came, men were digging again in the woods below the house. The cat waited patiently on the rise, hoping a mole might be unearthed for his supper. Once the hole was dug, the long black car would slink like a rat snake up the drive, winding through the wildflowers and the man's contraptions in the field, and men dressed black as crows would slide a long box from the back, shoulder it down the wooded hill, and plant it in the little garden of stones.

The cat had watched this doggy ritual before: first, long ago, as a kitten, when the old couple lived in the farmhouse. The old woman had left him saucers of milk on the porch, but the saucers stopped once the first box was buried. Later, the old man disappeared when the crows buried a second box beside the first. Then the man who lived in the house now had come, and the digging and burying stopped until last summer, when the crows came back and helped the man put a third box in the ground.

The cat turned to the sound of crunching gravel and watched the black car snake across the field. As before, dark-clad men wrestled a long box down the hill and sank it into the earth with ropes, then left the diggers to fill the hole like dogs burying an enormous bone.

Once they'd all gone, the cat crept down the hill, squeezed under the fence, and leapt onto the dirt mound. Overhead a redbird sang for a mate and a squirrel hurled itself from branch to branch in the canopy of trees. The cat breathed in the rare quiet.

The man—big, growling, a noise with dirt on it—had driven off before dawn. Years ago, when the man had arrived with his screaming machines and piles of metal clattering in the trailer behind his truck, the cat had fled to the woods. Now, older and slower, he found advantage in the man's odd ways.

True, the man daily drowned the quiet, hammered and pounded in his shop, made fire and sparks, forged huge twisted creatures that chased their tails when the wind provoked them. He barked and swore as he worked, hurled his tools across the yard, went silent only when he slept, and that seldom.

But the man kept clear of the woods the cat loved, shunned the creek, cold and thirst-quenching, to the south, and left the high weeds where the cat hunted and hid when raccoons, hunters, or the wild boy trespassed on the land. Best of all, the man left the crawlspace under the house open, and the cat slept by the furnace in winter and lay in the cool earth there on hot summer days. But since the last moon the man and his helper had begun to fix, mow, and prune the place, and the cat sensed that his life was about to change.

He heard the roar of the man's truck in the drive, and soon after, the rustle of leaves above him. He ducked behind a stone. A child—small and wild-haired with big, curious eyes—stood on the rise, haloed in a blaze of sun. She lingered, staring, but hearing the man call, she headed back across the field toward the house.

The cat followed her at a distance, keeping hidden in the weeds. She waved at the man on the farmhouse porch and startled a flock of goldfinches feeding atop the wildflower blooms. The birds rose skyward in a chittering burst, and her astonished gaze followed their flight. She took in the landscape as the cat would: the rising wind, gathering clouds, a change in the air. The outward signs that she noticed these things were subtle, but he caught them: a flare of nostril, the twitch of an ear, a slight shift of her wide eyes. She looked like a stray, alone in the world, as he was. He liked how she acknowledged the man but kept apart. How feline of her, he thought, how cat.

The man took himself sweating and panting into the house. Explosions of rapping, tapping, whirring, and buzzing poured from the open upstairs windows, irritating the day. The man crossed back and forth in front of the windows, huffing, puffing, and cursing, shouldering lengths of wood, as if he were felling a whole forest inside the house.

The girl called up: You okay, Uncle Henry? You want me to call 9-1-1?

The man snapped back: I'm fine! This house is an ancient piece of junk! Hardly fit for a man, much less a child!

I could help you if you want. I know about fixing things.

Don't be stupid, the man shouted, and went back to work.

The girl stomped into the field, ripping wildflowers off their roots with both fists, muttering: Stupid! Nearly twelve and still I got to deal with grown-ups too dumb to see I can do for myself! Did fine with a crazy mama and no daddy, and I don't need him!

The cat took in her meaning through every pore and trailed her back across the field, drawn as a thirst to water. The wind was picking up, and her hair blew about her angry face. She stormed over the rise and down the hill into the woods, but once inside the little fence she grew still and solemn. She set one fistful of flowers on the mounded dirt and the other against a carved stone beside it.

Hey, Daddy, she told the stone. Sorry we never met. And to the fresh-dug earth she said: Bye, Mama. You got your wish.

The air was heavy and cool and smelled of rain. Winds tossed the treetops, thunder sounded, and lightning veined the sky. Unafraid, the girl roamed the open field and scowled at each of the man's makings while the cat followed in secret. Near the house she stopped and lifted her nose, as though she caught his scent on the air. She stared straight at his hiding place, then turned suddenly and ran inside. The screen door slammed, and that instant it poured.

I'd hoped for better, Henry's being a heart doctor. A job like that, you'd think he might actually have a heart.

As usual, I pushed the cart down the aisle myself, taking what I needed off the shelves, the new grown-up as useless as those before him. Negative help, as Mama's friend Manny used to say, negative being less than none. No big deal. Grocery shopping and I were old friends, along with toilet scrubbing, vacuuming, and wash.

Said grown-up—my before-last-Monday-never-heard-of uncle Henry—trailed behind, scowling and muttering, not seeming to know what to do with himself, alternating between keeping five or six paces back like I was contagious and breathing down my neck in the unlikely event I needed him for something. I wondered why he'd claimed me at all.

At first I thought he'd been charitable to adopt me just shy of a foster home and kind to bury Mama, seeing how she wasn't even his kin. I mean, isn't that what every orphan dreams of? A big, strong, important man to swoop in at the last hour and say, "Don't worry, darling girl, I'll be your new daddy. I'll take care of every little thing." Yeah, right.

For the two days I'd known Henry Augustus Royster, my half-uncle on my daddy's side, he'd been irritation in the flesh—fidgety and frowning, taking his big, grimy hands in and out of his even grimier jeans pockets, rubbing his red-gray beard or the red bandanna tied around his bald head, adjusting his wire-rimmed glasses, eyeing the exits and looking sore when I caught him. Plotting his escape already, I could tell. No different from Lester or Manny, Charlie, Harlan, or Ray. None of them had stuck. Neither would he.

"Be sure to get whatever you want," he said for the forty-third time. At least he was buying, unusual in adults of my acquaintance. "Anything at all."

"Okay," I said, testing him. "Run get me a twelve-pack of beer and a carton of cigarettes. *Lights*," I added. "I need to cut down."

"You don't smoke or drink," he scoffed. "You're only eleven years old."

"Sneaking up on twelve. And I've cut way back," I said, studying the cereal shelf. "Used to be a real chimney when I was six."

I suspected he had a good laugh inside him, but it was hidden under an outside as prickly as a cactus. He just glared.

I glared right back. "You wouldn't know a joke if it bit you on the butt."

"Is that so?"

"Bet you're a Cancer."

"What?"

"Your astrological sign. Sign of the crab."

"Do tell."

"Like I said."

He was big-chested, muscular, and okay handsome for a fossil of fifty-some. He dressed strange for an old man, though: muscle shirts, dirty jeans, heavy boots, a bandanna or rag tied around his bald head, and a ruby stud in one earlobe like a pirate. His upper arms were as big around as fence posts, and he could've picked me up easy with one catcher's-mitt-sized hand. He had a belly, but it looked good on him, made him seem sturdy, like he could stand a storm. He'd be better looking if he laughed, though, and I decided to make it my personal mission to loosen him up.

"I got to be a regular chain-smoker by the time I was eight," I said, switching the subject back, "but it was cutting my wind, hurting my kickball game."

Henry smirked.

"Reach me one of those raisin brans on the top shelf," I told him, pointing up at the cereal boxes. He was more tolerable when he had an activity to distract him, something to do with his hands, like when Mama'd made potholders and ashtrays at the hospital to keep her mind off being mental.

"What else?" he said impatiently.

I headed down the health and beauty aisle toward the shampoos, and felt him take in my scrawny self: jeans, T-shirt, flip-flops, the major mane of curly red hair that no amount of conditioner ever tamed. It was the exact same color as the red parts of Henry's beard. Okay, so we had one thing in common.

"I'm getting the good kind, since you're buying."

"Whatever."

I took down the pricey brand and glanced back. He'd tossed six or eight more boxes of cereal in the cart, all the raisin bran on the shelf. I'd read artists were weird, but Henry was starting to worry me. Last thing I needed was Mama all over again.

A woman shopper came down the aisle and smiled flirtatiously at him as she passed. He snarled, I swear.

"Regular meat market in here," I said, loud so she'd hear. "That's the fourth time that's happened."

Like it or not, Henry drew people's attention. He didn't have to try. I saw it first thing when he picked me up at the social worker's office at the hospital in Farmville. Something drew people to him whether they wanted to go or not. And not just women, everybody. The minute Henry walked in, even the two doped-up patients watching *Oprah* turned to stare at him. The feeling in the room changed, became kind of exciting, like something important and a little dangerous was about to happen. When he spoke, his deep voice made you listen, even if he was just ordering a cup of coffee or asking where he might find his niece, Ms. Zoë Royster. *Ms.*—I liked that. Thing was, his power mixed in with his cranky nature made me think of a ticking time bomb, and more than once since yesterday I'd thought to run and hide.

"I saw in *People* magazine that good-looking doctors rate number one on the list of best catches," I said, trying to lighten the conversation. But Henry's expression darkened, told me it was the wrong thing to say.

"I don't practice medicine much anymore," he said, like he was spitting out something rotten.

"Too bad. You'd be good at it. A disease would take one look at you and fly out the door."

"Is that a fact?"

"That look alone might cure cancer. I read that a person's moods can kill or cure, depending."

His eyes narrowed like I'd hit a nerve. "Is there anything you don't know or haven't read?"

"I read a lot. But most of that magazine stuff's bogus. Junk food for your brain. You know, 'Hubble Telescope Sights Elvis on Mars.' That kind of thing."

"So why do you read them?"

"Oh, I don't *read* them," I said, trying to decide if I wanted jasmine body lotion or honeysuckle. "I look at the headlines while I wait at the checkout. They're funny and they pass the time and tell you about people."

He looked doubtful. "For instance?"

"Oh, what makes people happy. What worries them. What they're scared of."

"So what makes people happy?"

"True love."

"What worries them?"

"That they won't ever find it."

"And what scares them?"

"That maybe they will."

I picked the jasmine lotion and looked back over my shoulder. Henry was studying me like adults do, like I was smarter than he'd thought, like I knew too much for a kid. I remembered what I'd overheard the hospital social worker tell him.

"Zoë's street smarts are a kind of armor she wears to protect herself," she'd said, making me sound like an armadillo. "She's taken care of herself since she was old enough to walk. Her mother spent more time in mental hospitals than not, and Zoë's father—your half-brother, I gather—left right after conception. Over the years, Zoë's lived in the neglectful and permissive care of one or another of her mother's boyfriends, or, occasionally, alone. Under the circumstances, she's an extraordinary child."

Imagine that. Me, extraordinary.

"You look funny," I said to Henry. I was tired of everybody scrutinizing me like something under a microscope.

"I was just trying to decide if there's a tiny, smart-mouthed grown-up zipped inside your sneaking-up-on-twelve-year-old body."

"Yeah? You gonna look inside my ears with your doctor flashlight when we get back?"

"I might."

He followed me to the pet-food aisle, and started eyeballing me again while I was deciding which kind of cat food to buy. I chose the one with four different flavors and set it in the cart. He looked at me like I was touched in the brain.

"*What?*" I said, with as much attitude as I could muster.

"What's the cat food for?" he asked, as though I was planning to eat it myself.

"Oh, gosh, let's see." I drummed my cheek with my fingertips and rolled my eyes toward the ceiling. "What would cat food be for? That's a hard one. Cat food. Oh yeah, it's for the cat," I said, flashing a fake smile, trying not to let my voice show what a doofus he was.

"I don't have a cat."

I studied his face. He really didn't know. An animal slept, hunted, and ate not twenty yards from his front door and he didn't have one clue. What was it with grown-ups, anyway? Life zipped right past them. "Oh, he's out there all right," I said. "Big as life."

"Out where?"

"In your *yard*," I said. I could not believe that the President of the United States had actually let Dr. Henry Royster cut him open. The article I'd read about it in the library was old, but it said that Henry graduated first in his class at the famous Johns Hopkins University Medical School, was a distinguished naval surgeon, and even operated on the President before leaving medicine "to become one of America's preeminent artists"—things your average moron did not usually do. Henry was looking at me funny again, probably wondering if, after everything I'd been through, my mind had snapped. The way people used to look at Mama. I didn't like this look. I didn't like it at all.

"You've actually seen this cat?"

I wheeled the cart into the paper-product aisle, trying to think how to explain it—the way I sometimes felt the presence of living things without actually seeing them. It would be impossible to explain to somebody this clueless. "He's there, all right. Betcha fifty dollars," I said. Adults take things more seriously when money is involved.

"What?"

"I'm good for it!"

"That's not what I meant."

"So?"

"You gamble?"

"*Sometimes*," I said. "Everybody gambles."

"I don't."

"Oh, right," I said. "Like when you *used* to cut people open, you always knew exactly how everything was going to work out."

Henry started to say something but then stopped and said, "Point taken."

"So, is it a bet?"

"Certainly not."

"Come on. Where's your sense of adventure?" I asked, climbing up two shelves to get the box of tissues with yellow butterflies on it.

Henry plucked me down, set me on the floor, snatched the box from my hand, and put it in the cart. "Do you ever let anybody do anything for you?"

"Not if I can help it."

"Why not?"

"I depend on myself, that's why," I said, "and don't change the subject. I won five hundred dollars at the track before I was seven."

"What track?"

"The *race*track. When I was living in New York with Mama and Manny. Manny said I knew how to pick 'em. I won nearly two thousand dollars total, the trifecta *twice*. Course, Manny had to place the bets for me, 'cause I wasn't old enough."

"Or tall enough to reach the window," he said. "So tell me, have you had kids yet?"

"I'm waiting till I'm married."

"Glad to hear it."

"So, is it a bet?"

"What did you do with all your money?"

"Spent it."

"On what?"

"Things," I told him. Most of my winnings had gone to pay past-due bills and rent on places one step up from a dump. Not to mention what Mama and her friends had "borrowed" from me before I'd learned to hide my winnings better. "I've always paid my own way, so don't worry."

Henry stared at me as if he was trying unsuccessfully to add me up on his mental calculator. "You said this fifty-dollar cat is a *he*. How do you know?"

"Double or nothin'?"

"How?" he insisted.

"You don't need to get close. Just like you don't need to get close to a man or a woman to tell which is which."

"I've been fooled on occasion." He lifted his eyebrows and made a you-wouldn't-believe-some-of-the-things-I've-seen face, and I had to chuckle.

Our conversation had attracted the attention of other shoppers. A good-sized crowd had gathered at one end of the aisle. They were craning around the canned goods, whispering to each other. The pitying way they looked at me was familiar, but I had the impression from how they looked at Henry that they didn't know what to make of him at all.

"Why are they staring at us like that?" I whispered.

"Small town," Henry said. "Fred usually does the shopping."

"Who's Fred?"

"You'll meet him tomorrow. He helps me take care of things around the place."

I turned to the people at the end of the aisle and shouted, "Y'all don't have to worry. He's not dangerous during the day."

For the first time since I'd met Henry Royster, he smiled, showing a gap between his two front teeth exactly like mine.

"I'll be," I said, staring at it. "We really *are* related."

The other shoppers looked away or wandered off, their invisible tails between their legs, except for one old lady in a black-and-white-striped dress who stood her ground, skunk-like.

Henry swore under his breath, full serious again.

I made a U-turn and headed for the detergents, Henry hard behind. "Extra strength," I said, looking at his nasty jeans.

He reached absently for an orange plastic bottle on the middle shelf, but I whispered, "They test on animals. Blue bottle," and pointed to a brand on a lower shelf. Henry obliged.

"You like animals," he said, some warmer.

"Their love's purer," I said.

"Than?"

"People's. That's what Mrs. King used to say."

"Mrs. King?"

"She's who taught me to read and write, and other things too, till her heart gave out. Lived next door to me and Lester."

"Lester?"

"Lester's who took care of me and Mama before Manny. I'm writing it all down in my memoir."

"Aren't you a little young to write your life story?"

"A lot's happened to me! Besides, I used to read them all the time to Charlie's mama. She was blind. Mrs. King taught me reading, but Charlie's mama was how I got good at it. Memoirs and murder mysteries were her favorites. She said her life was dull as red dirt and she lived life through people in books."

"Who's Charlie?"

"Charlie mowed people's yards. He was Mama's boyfriend between Manny and Harlan, who was her next to last. Harlan fixed cars and taught me to drive, stick, standard, and column. Want me to drive home? I'm good at it."

"Next to last?" Henry asked.

"Before Ray. Ray was Mama's last boyfriend. My keeper before you."

Henry frowned at Ray's name. Ray had that effect on people, especially me. I was glad Henry didn't ask any more.

We came out of the aisle and saw the other shoppers gabbing near the checkout. Skunk Woman stood in front. Madame Buttinsky, I thought, Nosy Parker Club President.

"Everything all right, Doctor?" she said crisply, emphasis on the word *Doctor.* "It's been some time since we've seen you in town." She studied us up and down the way a mean mama would look at her kids. "We're all sorry for your loss, dear," she went on, shifting her disapproval to me and not sounding sorry one bit.

"Mrs. Wilson," Henry said stiffly. He put his hand on my shoulder and squeezed. "This is my niece, Zoë. She's come to live with me."

Mrs. Wilson looked as though she thought this an extremely questionable idea.

"Nice of him, too," I told her, "seeing how I've served hard time."

Henry squeezed my shoulder till it hurt, but I didn't let on. I wouldn't have given him or Skunk Woman the satisfaction.

"I see that mendacity and smart tongues run deep in the Royster family," said Mrs. Wilson, "alongside promiscuity and godless ways."

I could've spit fire. "I know what those words mean, you cussed old—" I said, fixing to tell her where she could stick her opinions, but Henry cut me off.

"We'll be going now, Mrs. Wilson. My regards to Dr. Wilson," he said, scooping me up under one stinky armpit and rushing me and the cart toward the checkout.

"You gonna take that from her?" I shouted. "She called us tramps and liars!"

"Zip it," was all he said.

Make me, would've been the next words out of my mouth, but his sharp tone seemed like the fuse on a stick of dynamite I didn't want to light.

We rode back to Henry's without talking, both of us stewing.

I was too mad and tired to care which of his bad moods Henry was in or why. He had to be the moodiest person I'd ever met, Mama and her friends included.

I thought about all the Mrs. Wilsons I'd known, all the busybodies who'd wanted to say who was fit to raise me and who wasn't, always turning up their noses at me and my life. If Henry held such views, at least he kept them to himself. He slipped a CD in the dash—a slow, suffering kind of music with no singing. He turned it up loud.

I took the hint and looked out the truck window, taking in Sugar Hill in all its squalor, no sweetness in sight. Mama and I'd lived in a dozen towns just like it, towns that except for a couple of fast-food places or a car dealership didn't look like part of the twenty-first century. Block after block, storefronts stood empty, with dusty For Rent signs hanging crooked in the windows or doors. Here and there, a laundromat or pawnshop or liquor store struggled between the ramshackle houses and dusty yards of the dirt poor and always tired. There were little markets or *tiendas* with handwritten specials in the windows. Kids ran through sprinklers to keep cool or played in the street after the cars passed, and older folks gathered on corners or porches waiting for the sun to go down and take the heat with it. More than a few people smiled and waved happily at the sight of Henry, but Henry was too inside his own head to see. Put out as I was at Henry, I liked that he was friendly with the have-not side of town.

We passed the lawyers' offices that divided the poor and rich neighborhoods. Beyond them, bigger houses had shady patios and screened porches. Flowers spilled from hanging baskets, and the shrubbery was shorn into perfect rounds or squares. A mile later we were in the country, headed back to Henry's.

Thank the Lord the phone rang as we were putting away the groceries, and Henry stormed down the hall to his study to answer it. I climbed the kitchen stepladder and took down two bowls, then filled one with cat food and one with water. I slipped an aluminum pie plate under my arm like a Frisbee and carried it and the bowls outside. The heavy summer darkness oozed over the yard like molasses. I welcomed the end of this particular day.

I set the bowls on the stoop and filled the pie plate with water from the spigot on the house. I carried it carefully to a low, wooden crate I'd set sideways at the edge of the yard and put it inside. Then I went back for the two bowls and placed the food bowl inside the pie plate the way Mrs. King had taught me. The water in the pie plate made a moat around the food bowl and kept the ants out.

"If you don't like that kind, I'll get you something else," I said in the direction of the weeds. "Just don't eat it and I'll know." I kept my voice soft and moved slowly. If I spooked or startled him now, he might never trust me. I felt him watching me, but I couldn't pick him out in the darkness. "You're a good hider. That's important."

"Zoë!"

Henry's heavy boots clomped on the porch floorboards. The porch bulb snapped on, flooding the yard with light. Henry Royster, one-man herd of rhinos. He stood on the steps, hands on his hips, shouting that there were sandwiches in the refrigerator. I adjusted my eyes to the glaring brightness, then stepped into the light, waving both arms over my head so he'd know I was all right. I didn't want him thundering out here, scaring the wildlife for twenty miles. The phone rang again, and I was glad he headed back inside.

"Don't worry, I'm working on him," I whispered to the weeds, and walked back to the house to turn off that obnoxious light.

I flipped the switch, and the night came back, soft and restful. Once my eyes readjusted to the dark, I looked up to see stars burning bright overhead. Stargazing would be one good thing about living out here in the country with Henry, I thought, imagining Orion buckling on his sparkly belt before the night's hunt and the big and little bear swimming together around the planets.

As I came in, I heard Henry talking on the phone in his study.

"She's outside taking food to an imaginary cat she bet me fifty dollars is living out there in the grass. . . . Don't you think I'd know if a cat was living out there? . . . What do you mean by that? . . . Well, Fred, I never knew you thought I was such a dimwitted old fool. . . ."

I smiled at this as I climbed the stairs, catching a glimpse of Henry surrounded by a desk littered with papers and floor-to-ceiling walls of books. Next to animals, I loved books more than anything, and for a minute I imagined myself staying in this place, so big and different from the stuffy apartments, cramped houses, and tin-can trailers I'd lived in before. I imagined having my very own room instead of a sleeping bag or a made-up sofa, a book I could keep longer than two weeks if I wanted, and a grown-up smarter than I was in the house. I imagined having all that for a whole minute before I remembered what it felt like to hope for things I'd never get. I pushed the wanting away as hard as I could.

"Night, Uncle Henry," I called.

I got into my new bed with my clothes on, too tired to undress. I took my spiral notebook from the table drawer and made a few notes for my memoir. Too weary for fine words, I wrote, "Uncle Henry's got a big bug up his butt, but it's a more interesting bug than most."

A second later, Henry knocked.

"Come on in," I called, slipping the notebook under the covers. It was strange to have my very own door and a grown-up, however bad-tempered, with the manners to knock.

"I came to say good night," he said from the doorway. I recognized the heaviness in his voice. Weight crept into all their voices once they'd had a taste of parenting and got to thinking how much work and responsibility a kid was, how much of their precious time I was going to suck up, how I'd hold them back, mess up their plans, how I didn't have an off switch they could flip every time they wanted to get on with their screwed-up lives. Usually the heaviness took a week or so to seep in, but our meeting in a mental ward, burying Mama, and running into Skunk Woman had made the last two days more trying than most.

"Night, Uncle Henry," I said again.

"I have to see to a few things tomorrow," he said. "I'll be leaving well before you're up and late coming back."

My heart fluttered. I breathed deep and tried to calm it, but when the heart knows the truth there's no telling it lies. That was just the kind of thing they all said before takeoff, stage one in the ditch-the-kid countdown. Three: The lame excuse announcing the all-day or all-night errand. Two: The weeklong trip to help a needy friend or tend a dying relation. One: The job out of state that would take as long as it took. Then blastoff.

"It can't be helped," Henry said, looking out my window at the night.

Can't look me in the eye, I thought, another telling sign. "Whatever," I said.

"Fred'll come as soon as he can get here in the morning. He and his wife, Bessie, live up the road, and he helps me around here. I'll leave his phone number on the kitchen table."

Sure you will, I thought.

Henry stood in the doorway, backlit by the hall light. He seemed to be trying to think of something else to say, something to make both of us feel easier about things.

"I'm used to it," I told him.

"What?"

"To people coming and going," I said. "To being on my own. Been on my own pretty much my whole life. After a while, you get used to it, even get to liking it."

Another long silence. Henry bowed his head and I heard his breathing, felt him turning over what I'd said in his mind.

"Bull," he said, and shut the door behind him.

2

I woke up early the next morning, but not early enough. I raced to the landing windows overlooking the front yard. The sun barely haloed the treetops, but Henry's pickup was already gone.

I headed downstairs in the humid near-dark wearing the clothes I'd slept in. The stairs dipped in the middle with the wear of years, and I closed my eyes and thought about their history. Henry's mama and daddy had lived here, and more of our kin before that. I pictured generations of my relations climbing up and down: young and old, red-haired, gap-toothed, and pigheaded.

In the kitchen I filled a big mug halfway with coffee, lifted the chipped lid off the sugar bowl, and put in my customary eight spoonfuls. Then I filled the cup the rest of the way with milk. Henry had set a place for me with a bowl and spoon, a box of raisin bran, and—wonder of wonders—a note with Fred's phone number. *Back tonight,* it said. He'd signed his whole name, *Henry Royster,* and then he'd crossed out *Royster* and wedged *Uncle* in front of *Henry.*

I found my turkey sandwich from the night before in the refrigerator, wrapped it in a napkin, and took it with my coffee to look around. There'd been no time for exploring yet. You can tell a lot about people by studying how they live, and today I aimed to nose around in case Henry came back.

Unlike other places I'd lived, Henry's house had lots of windows and good light. Mama'd lived in the dark, like a mole. When she wasn't in the hospital or working some scrape-by job, she'd kept to her bedroom during the day with the shades drawn and the door locked. Once in a while I honestly forgot she was there. I'd be reading or drawing in whatever corner of the place was mine, and suddenly she'd shuffle by, thin and pale and red-eyed in her dirty nightgown and bedroom slippers, her hair mashed flat on one side and her dark roots showing. A few minutes later she'd shuffle back the other way, ghostlike, which is how I came to think of her. She'd whisper "Hey, baby" as she passed, if she noticed me at all. The only times she'd put on a little makeup and come to life was at night or between boyfriends. Once she'd snagged a man, she bothered less and less till he was gone.

Lester was the first live-in I remember, though I have hazy memories of other suckers before that. He worked hard, sometimes ten and twelve hours a day, but the center of his at-home universe was a recliner and a color TV ringed with overflowing ashtrays, a twelve-pack or more of crumpled beer cans, and assorted bags of pretzels, popcorn, and corn chips—his idea of a high time.

The only thing bigger than Manny's TV were his stereo

speakers. Our neighbors in the apartments on either side were always banging on our walls and yelling for him to pipe down, which he did, but only to make bets or order pizza. Every inch of the living room was papered in sports sections and racing forms, balled up or torn to confetti when he lost, which was most of the time.

Harlan and Charlie were champion sleepers, twelve to fourteen hours a day if they could manage it, which was the only way anybody could spend quality time with Mama. Ray was a shedder. Everything lay exactly where he took it off or tired of it, like a snake slithering out of its skin.

But Henry's house was clean and airy, with none of the trash I was used to and no TV in sight. Bedsheets covered the sofa, chairs, tables, lamps, and cardboard boxes in the closed-off front room.

The front hallway told me that a working man lived here. A sledgehammer leaned against the wall at the foot of the stairs with a cardboard box of nuts and bolts beside it. Grimy work clothes hung on pegs, and a line of scuffed and muddy boots sat underneath, all smelling of grease and sweat, the smell of every man who'd cared for me since I was a tiny child. But Henry's likeness to them stopped there. The sun was up by now, and I went back up the stairs, studying the pictures that lined the walls and thinking Henry was like no working man I'd ever known.

Thirty, maybe forty drawings and paintings were tacked up one after the other—and sometimes one on top of the other—from the ceiling to the paint-spattered floor. They were good, too. Many were of the same woman with long brown hair—a drawing of her face and hands, one of her glancing over her bare shoulder, one of her in profile, looking thoughtful—all sketched with just a few lines. There were other pictures without her: painted blocks of colors that seemed to float off the wall into the air and pictures of overlapping circles, triangles, and squares done in bright, thick paint. And sometimes the pencil, crayon, or brushstrokes went off the paper right onto the wall.

On the second-floor landing outside my room a shiny silver mobile floated above me like indoor clouds. Up the stairs to the third floor dozens more pictures cluttered the walls on both sides. I touched the actual marks and felt the rough surface of the paint. If my blood relative had drawn and painted these, I might have ability myself. Henry's pictures were full of color and life. Maybe some of that life might rub off on me.

On the third floor I opened the door to Henry's room and stood amazed at what I saw. It was one humongous space. Each long wall had a bank of four arched floor-to-ceiling windows, pointed at the top like the windows in a church. Near me stood a huge drawing table, its slanted top cluttered with taped-down notes and sketches. Beside it was a rolling chair, an empty easel, a table with sets of oil paints and pastels in wooden boxes, and jars of brushes, their handles covered with dried colors but their upended bristles clean. Above the drawing board were dozens more pictures, sketches of sculptures I'd seen in the yard, and more pictures of the woman—though in these she looked thinner, and her hair was cropped short or covered with a scarf.

Overhead, a dozen mobiles dangled and swirled from hooks in the high ceiling. A mobile of butterflies and silver birds spun over the drawing table. Another one of red, blue, and yellow circles and triangles whirled above my head.

At the far end of the room was an enormous bed that looked like something from a fairy tale. Its four posters reached nearly to the ceiling, each one made from metal into the trunk of a slender tree from one of the four seasons. Autumn's and summer's branches intertwined to form a headboard with *Henry loves Mandy* written along it in silver script. Mandy must be the woman in the pictures. I wondered where she was now.

The bed was unmade and the room messy in a comfortable, lived-in way, though clean and cared for underneath. Books were everywhere. They littered the bed and floor, teetered ten and twelve high on the two bedside tables, leaned against one another on the windowsills and the dresser, even spilled out of the open dresser drawers. Wobbly stacks sagged an old sofa that couldn't have been sat on unless you were a mouse. For sitting, there was a single armchair and a footstool, but even there, books lay open over the chair's armrests and back.

Even more wonderful, there weren't any library markings on the spines, no red-inked *Property Of* stamps on the closed pages, no *Due Back in 14 Days* stickers inside the back covers. Henry *owned* each and every book. Most were about artists. I admired their covers, whispered the titles, and tried to work out the artists' strange names: Picasso, Gonzales, Man Ray, Rothko, Archipenko, Serra, Klee, Kapoor, Arp, Giacometti, di Suvero, Bontecou, and Miró.

I stood in the middle of this magic for a long while, taking it all in. Maybe this room was why the people in town looked at Henry like he'd gone round the bend. Folks were probably thinking: *Who'd be crazy enough to give up being a rich and famous doctor to live like this?* But I knew about crazy. I'd lived with true craziness all my life, and nothing this beautiful or joyful had ever come from it. This was the total opposite of crazy.

A drawing pad rested beside a box of pencils, erasers, and charcoal on the bed. I fingered the pencils, suddenly itching to draw pictures of my own. I lifted the cover of the pad and saw a drawing of an upside-down face. I turned it right side up, thinking to see another picture of the woman Henry was forever drawing. When I saw who it was, an ant could've knocked me over, easy. There, drawn in pencil, in eight or ten perfect lines, was a picture of *me*.

I closed the cover on the pad and went down to the second floor. My own room seemed disappointing now, though it was the best of the three rooms on the floor. There was a small wooden sleigh bed that had belonged to Henry when he was a boy, a mirrored dresser, an empty old steamer trunk that smelled like mothballs, and a walk-in closet. Four high windows overlooked the backyard and had a roomy, cushioned window seat underneath. I'd opened all the windows to let in air, but I'd left my suitcase—a Piggly Wiggly paper bag—packed, just in case. Not that I had much: an extra pair of jeans, three T-shirts, a jacket, four pairs of socks, some raggedy underclothes, and a skirt with the last of my emergency fund—a rubber-banded roll of fifty-three one-dollar bills—stuffed into a pocket. I set my drugstore notebook and pencils on the window seat, and put my old brown bunny, missing an ear, on the covers of the bed. Enough moving in. Odds were I'd be moving out before long.

I headed downstairs to Henry's study, which I'd saved for last. Walls of books rose from the floor to the old tin ceiling, and there was a ladder on wheels for climbing up to the topmost shelves. I inhaled the musty, leathery, old-papery scent and a shiver passed over me. If I had any idea of heaven, it was this: shelves and shelves of books, ten times as many as were upstairs, each with stories or pictures more exciting and beautiful than the next, and two overstuffed chairs big enough for me to sleep in.

In every place Mama and I had landed, I'd made the town library my true home. Summers and weekends were the best times, because I could spend the whole day there in heated or air-conditioned quiet. During the school year, I took care not to show up before three in the afternoon, so nobody would know I played hooky. But after three, I could stay till closing time, usually eight or nine o'clock. No matter how sick Mama got or what low-life she took up with, no matter what worried my mind, books made me feel better.

In Henry's library, I counted ten shelves from floor to ceiling on each long wall, one bookcase on each side of the three tall windows on the sunrise side, and two more on either side of the double doors to the hall. I tested his big leather chair, leaning way back, then twirling and twirling until I was dizzy. Dust motes danced on the sunrays that shone slantwise across the room. I whirled in the warm light and breathed the book-scented air.

The shelves held titles I knew: *Treasure Island, Robin Hood, Rascal, The Animal Family*. I touched the familiar spines but lingered a longer time on books I'd never seen before, taking out one with pictures about a Japanese boy who drew cats. Inside the front cover it said: *Henry Royster, age 8*. I slipped the small book into my waistband and felt a sudden sinking in my stomach as Ray's creepy, naysaying voice started up in my head. "Who you kidding, little girl? You ain't nothing. You ain't never going to be nobody. Gimme a dollar," he'd sneer every time he caught me reading or writing in my notebook. Then he'd laugh and laugh. Suddenly I felt like a street kid looking in a candy-store window, watching other kids with mamas and daddies buying them whatever they liked. "Give it up, darling," Ray snickered between my ears. "Ain't none of this ever gonna be yours."

I shook off the feeling and looked at the things on Henry's desk: a laptop computer, the screen dark; two open magazines about doctoring; piles and more piles of papers and files; a heap of opened and unopened mail; more sketchpads with doodles all over them, drawing pencils, and pencil shavings. On one corner and about to avalanche was a foot-tall stack of magazines with names like *Sculpture, Artforum,* and *ARTnews.*

On top of the pile was the latest issue of *Art International* magazine with a cover picture of a younger, scowling Henry and the headline *WHERE'S ROYSTER? The Disappearing American Master.* I was reaching for it when I spied a large checkbook lying open in the middle of the desk. The last entry jolted me like an electric shock: *Rose Hill Hospital, $5,450.* Rose

Hill was the hospital where they rushed Mama in the ambulance, the place where she died.

"I knocked, but nobody answered," said a voice from the doorway.

I jumped, and the magazines and my empty coffee mug fell to the floor, the mug shattering. A silver-haired man with milk-chocolate skin as wrinkly as a walnut shell peered around the open door. He had a wide, friendly face and wore overalls with all manner of tools spilling out of the pockets.

"I'm Fred, Fred Montgomery. You must be Zoë."

"You scared the spit out of me," I said.

"Teach you to go nosing." He shot me a sly look and nodded at the papers on Henry's desk.

"Just investigating my new circumstances. You gonna tell?"

Fred looked insulted. "Heck no. Relief to know somebody around here's nosier than I am."

I waited, not sure what to say. He seemed nice enough, but so had every one of Mama's friends at first, even Ray.

"My wife, Bessie, and I live a mile or so on," he said. "Walking distance for those with young legs."

"Henry said you help him."

"That's right."

"Like a handyman?"

"Handyman. Cook. Bottle-washer. Assistant lifter, hauler, welder, and grinder. Henry calls me his right hand, but that's too high-sounding for me. Had your breakfast?"

I nodded.

"Want more of what was in that cup?" he asked, glancing at the pieces on the floor.

"I guess."

"Juice? Milk?"

"Coffee."

He smiled, shook his head. "Well, you pick up the pieces while I fire up a fresh pot."

By the time I was done, Fred had the coffee brewing and two mugs waiting on the counter. "I'm real sorry about your mama," he said as I came in the kitchen. "Your daddy, too. Sorry for the whole mess."

"Thanks," I told him, looking away, not wanting to talk about it.

He leaned back on the counter and turned to look out the window. "I hear we have a trespasser."

"Trespasser?"

"A fifty-dollar trespasser."

"The cat!" I pulled a chair over to the sink, climbed up, and squinted out the window at the front yard, but Fred's candy-apple-red pickup truck blocked my view. I whistled.

"That's my office," he said proudly. "Like it?"

"I can drive," I said, cutting my eyes his way.

"So I hear." He poured the coffee and handed me a cup, then watched as I took it to the table and added my eight sugars and some milk. "You were saying? About the cat."

"I haven't actually seen him, so Henry doesn't believe me. But he's out there. He's been out there a while."

"What makes you say that?"

"Lester called it a sense I have for animals. My seventh sense."

"Who's Lester?"

"One of Mama's friends."

"Friends?"

I sat on my knees in a kitchen chair, elbows on the table, stirring my coffee, watching it swirl. "That's what she called the men who liked to take her out, took care of her when she didn't feel good, and minded me when she was in the hospital. Mama was real pretty, so she made friends easy, but she was real crazy, so they didn't last long. Lester worked nights at a vet place and let me sit with the boarded animals while he cleaned up."

Fred turned to wash the dishes. I offered to help, but he said it sounded as if I'd been cleaning up after grown-ups since the day I was born and I'd earned a rest. "You got other talents besides your gift with animals?" he asked.

"Manny taught me to pay Mama's bills and figure out her checkbook. And Charlie taught me how to prune and mow."

"Those aren't talents, those are chores!" Fred said over his shoulder.

"What do you mean? I'm good at them!"

"Well, fine, but there's a difference between a chore and a talent. Chores are what you *have* to do. Talents are your natural abilities, what believers like Bessie would call your gifts from God. Things you're good at without knowing why."

I'd never considered the difference.

Fred saw my confusion. "You know Henry used to be a doctor?"

"I read about it at the library. He operated on the President."

"That's right. A heart surgeon. He operated on Bessie's heart after he moved back here. Did it for nothing, too."

"I thought he quit doctoring."

"Mostly. He still keeps up his license, though, looks after Bessie and a few others at the free clinic in town. But don't say where you heard that."

I zipped my lips.

"Anyway," Fred went on, "Henry was a good doctor, but that's what Henry's daddy, Augustus, wanted him to be."

"My grandfather?"

"That's right. Stern fella, Augustus. Not a man you said no to."

"You knew him?"

Fred nodded. "Bessie and I grew up here, same as Henry. Everybody knew Augustus and his temper. That man would fuss if you hung him with a new rope."

"What's that mean?"

"Somebody who complains about everything, even things that don't matter."

I saw now. Born griping. Like Ray.

"Anyway," Fred went on, "when he was growing up, everybody could see Henry was good at art, except Augustus. To please his daddy, Henry joined the Navy, went to medical school, and became a fine doctor. But it didn't make him happy. So after a while he left doctoring and went back to making art. Good art, too. Had people lined up clear to China to buy it. He fell into a little slump, but he's coming back."

"What kind of slump?"

Fred's voice softened. "His wife died."

So that's who was in all the drawings and paintings.

"He didn't tell you?"

I shook my head.

"When Henry first came back, I hadn't seen him since we were kids. Doc Wilson was out seeing Bessie, and he said he didn't know why I'd called *him* when I had one of the country's best heart specialists living right next door. I drove over and found Henry raging over a flat tire on his trailer, throwing things and cursing to wake the dead. I turned my truck around and hollered, 'Give me a call when you're civil!'"

"Over a *tire?*" I asked.

"He was wound tight after his wife passed. He's not easy under the best circumstances, but that put him over the top. Can't say I'd be different if anything ever happened to Bessie. Scares me to think."

"What happened then?"

"He called the next day to apologize and said he'd do whatever he could for Bessie, though aside from a transplant he couldn't do much. Bessie was really the one who took care of Henry. She saw how he was and hired him to make a sculpture for the church. Or, as she says, 'to do what he was born to do.'"

Fred set the broom and dustpan in the closet and eyed the cat-food bag. "So what else were you born to do besides feed stray cats?"

"Gosh, we got to talking and I forgot!" I grabbed the bag

and raced outside, toppling my kitchen chair. I ran across the lawn to the crate. Both bowls were empty. I studied the weeds. I couldn't see him, but I felt him watching.

I filled his food bowl and ran back into the house to get water. Fred pressed himself flat against the wall to keep out of my way.

"Wait!" he called, and I stopped. He walked to his truck and took a small foil-wrapped package off the front seat. He parted the foil and handed it to me. "We had catfish for supper. Saved a little piece after Henry called."

I filled the moat and water bowl and set the catfish on top of the food while Fred waited for me by his truck. He squinted at the weeds, trying to see. "You think he minds me being here?"

"Not as long as you keep your distance."

"Like certain people," Fred said, giving me a sidelong look. "Shall we go to town and give him a little space?"

I took the cat food back in the house and then climbed in the passenger side of the truck. I put on my seat belt and looked up, but Fred wasn't moving. He sat still as stone, staring out the driver's window at the crate, his index finger to his lips.

"Don't slam your door," he whispered. "Your friend is taking our bait."

He could taste her kindness in the sweetness of the water.

Usually he drank from the creek or puddles, from the natural bowls of ditches or stumps. Each had its particular flavor, some strong, others bitter, some gritty, some chalky with mud. He hadn't tasted water this delicious in a long time. How long? He had vague memories from long ago of the crazy old woman and the nearer time of the boy's mother, but like his rippling reflection in the creek water, they wouldn't come clear.

The bowl beside him was a complete strangeness. He sniffed at the still little creatures inside it. Some smelled like bird, but weren't bird;

some smelled like fish, but weren't fish. He kept his eyes on them as he sniffed, expecting one to wriggle or scurry any second. He tried batting them with his paw. Nothing. He batted harder, tipping the bowl, and some spilled on the ground. He crouched, waiting to pounce if one ran for cover, took wing, made a game of it, but they all stayed put.

He glanced up at the girl's window. He saw her shadow there, unmoving but unmistakably her. Without taking his eyes off her, he bent down to the bowl and took one of the strange creatures in his teeth, bit it, chewed, and swallowed. Then another and another, until the bowl was empty.

The next morning she left him something more delectable. There were fish in the creek below the man's house, but this was different, firm-fleshed, aromatic, savory.

He licked the last of it from his nose and whiskers and remembered the boy's mother. She had left him such tidbits before the boy was born, nearly the cat's whole lifetime ago. But the day she'd died bearing the boy, the cat had sworn off humans. Taking food from the girl was risky, he knew, but at his age he wasn't the hunter he used to be. He could always leave the food tomorrow or the next day, if it was even there at all. With humans, you couldn't count on anything. For now, though, he let himself be persuaded.

3

Henry came back near sundown, but it wasn't long before I was wishing he hadn't. At first he seemed okay, tired but civil, even forked over my fifty dollars when Fred testified he'd seen the cat.

"He's black and white and has a mustache!" I told him.

"Well, I haven't seen him with my own eyes, now have I?" Henry said.

"Fred saw him. Didn't you, Fred?"

Fred nodded. "Big fella. Must weigh twelve or thirteen pounds. Watched him swallow half a catfish from last night's supper."

Henry looked doubtful, like maybe we'd cooked up this story between us.

"And guess what else?" I said, waving the bills in the air. "I got arrested!"

"What?" Henry turned to Fred.

"Sheriff Bean put on a little show," Fred explained.

"It wasn't any show! I got fingerprinted and Fred had to pay a fine."

"Fine?" Henry asked.

"Twelve whole packs of Juicy Fruit," I told him.

"Sheriff Bean's quit tobacco again," Fred put in.

"I see," Henry said.

"He says if I get so much as a sprained ankle, he'll put you in jail and throw away the key!"

"There's justice for you," Henry muttered.

"And after that, I got released into Fred's custody and met the Padre and Bessie!"

"Bessie all right?" Henry asked.

"She had a fine day," Fred told him. "How about you?"

Henry sighed and looked grumpy. More so after Fred handed him a pile of phone messages, all from the same woman, who'd called three or four times since Fred and I had been back. Henry cursed and stormed off to his workshop out back the second he read her name.

I headed for my room. Past experience with angry grown-ups had taught me to get out of the line of fire. A few minutes later Fred's truck pulled out of the drive. Henry's machines started up out back and his miserable music blared. He'd forgotten all about me. I brushed my teeth, took up my notebook, and climbed into bed.

I looked at all the things Fred and I had charged to Henry on our trip into town, mostly clothes for the coming winter: a warm jacket, two sweaters, three pairs of jeans, and a half-dozen long-sleeved shirts in different colors. Not one item was a hand-me-down or thrift-store special with stained places or holes you had to tuck in or wear a sweater over so nobody saw.

Everything was really and truly new, still in the plastic pack-ages with price tags attached. A half-dozen pairs each of new socks and underwear sat on top of my dresser, and on the floor of my closet was a pair of new sneakers that didn't rub my heels or pinch my toes, alongside my prized new possession: a pair of red leather boots almost too beautiful to wear.

I lay back on the pillows remembering the good parts of the day, starting with the cat. He was big and black with a white bib and belly and four white feet, plus a triangle of white around his nose, and a black spot like half a mustache to one side. We sat in Fred's truck, still and quiet, watching him eat every bit of food, after which he looked up at us with sleepy green-gold eyes, licked his muzzle, and then lumbered back to his weeds.

Sheriff Bean's blue lights flashed behind us almost as soon as we left the drive. He was short and round and wore sunglasses and a cowboy hat with a star stuck to the front. He had a wart on the end of his nose that would've made me cross-eyed if it had been mine, and his teeth were tobacco-stained dark brown.

"Looks like we got us a couple of dangerous criminals," he said sternly, peering into the driver's side. Then he lifted his sunglasses and smiled his brown smile, and he and Fred laughed.

After Fred and I went shopping, we met him at the sheriff's department, where he fingerprinted me. He said it was just for fun, but I heard him whisper to Fred, "Now, if she ever goes missing, we'll have 'em on file."

He told me all four of his girls were grown now, and if I

took a dislike to Henry, he and Mrs. Bean had empty bedrooms waiting. Then Fred's cell phone rang and Fred looked worried, but it was only Bessie wondering where in the heck we were.

Fred and Bessie lived at the end of a long, winding drive planted on either side with sunflowers, zinnias, and marigolds. Around their big log cabin, all kinds of flowers in every color reached for the sky or tumbled out of the beds. The air was busy with bees, yellow and blue butterflies, and little green and red hummingbirds that zipped up, down, backward, and sideways through the air like a tiny flying circus. One even came and hovered within a foot of my nose, studying me. There were other birds, too, black-capped chickadees and sparrows and bright red cardinals, to name some I knew.

Fred said that he used to farm tobacco, but it didn't pay anymore.

"Now I just make the land beautiful for Bessie and sell flowers to the fancy flower markets. You wouldn't believe what people'll pay for a half-dozen sunflowers these days," he said.

"How much?"

"Five or six dollars, retail. Bessie says folks are starved for beauty."

"Huh." I'd never thought how a person might be hungry for beauty.

"Mostly the flowers give her something to look at. It's hard having to stay in bed."

"Henry can't fix her?" I asked.

"Not all the way. She wouldn't even consider the heart transplant he recommended."

"I bet he could do it."

"He offered, but that wasn't the point. Bessie believes a body's beating heart makes that person who they are, that if they took out her heart she wouldn't be herself anymore. She's sure she wouldn't recognize me without her own heart to tell her who I was. And she doesn't even want to think what might happen if she had a stranger's heart inside her."

I didn't know what to say. Bessie was an unusual thinker. Fred said, "I know that look, but there's no reasoning with somebody who believes such things. It's like trying to argue somebody out of believing in angels. And she believes in *them*, too."

He shook his head and parked the pickup behind an old sedan that didn't look like it had been driven in a while. A faded bumper sticker on its trunk read: *Driving under the Influence of the Holy Spirit.*

He saw me reading it. "That's Bessie," he said. "Just so you know."

We stepped into the homiest place I'd ever seen. A tiny old woman lay propped up in the four-poster bed in the center of the living room. All around it were big overstuffed chairs with patchwork quilts and plump pillows thrown over them. Curtains in multicolored patterns hung in the windows, like something out of the story of Aladdin. Lamps made of tinted glass threw colors onto the walls, and prisms hanging from the curtain rods made little shivering rainbows everywhere. A kitchen area to one side had a big wooden table with cushiony chairs all round, and on the other side of the room a huge claw-footed bathtub peeked out from behind a beaded curtain.

I could tell the old woman in the bed had been pretty when she was young. A sparkle seemed to come from inside her. Her eyes were almond-shaped and soft brown, and she wore a tie-dyed cloth around her hair like a turban. She was sewing on a quilt that was held tight by a big wooden hoop in her lap and talking a mile a minute to a pink-faced man with wisps of white hair combed over his balding pink head. He sat hunched up in one of the big chairs, his hands resting on the crook of a cane between his legs.

"Father," she said as her eyes lit on me, "I'm having a vision."

"Then I'm having it too," said the old man, turning stiffly in my direction. "I'm Father Philip."

"Mostly known as the Padre," Bessie added.

"I'd get up," he said, "but I'm old and decrepit."

"I'm Bessie, honey," the woman told me, smiling. She set her sewing down and reached toward me with both small hands, so I couldn't help but take them in mine.

"Zoë," I said.

She leaned forward and pressed my cheeks in her cool palms. She smelled like cinnamon. "I prayed and prayed for God to send me a child, and you look as if you could use some holy mothering. What on earth took you so long to get here?"

"I don't really know," I said.

She and Father Philip looked at each other and laughed, and Fred just stood there, shaking his head. "I'll make your tea," he told her, moving off into the kitchen.

"You made all these quilts?" I asked, settling in a big chair.

"Every one," she said. "Gives me something to do besides watch television and worry over the sorry state of people's souls."

"You let me worry about that," said the old man.

Bessie turned to me. "The Padre's having trouble with his sermon."

"You're a preacher?" I asked him.

"Apparently not," he said. "Not a good one, anyway."

"Our congregation's complaining," Bessie said. "They say he gives the same sermon every Sunday."

"And it's true, really," the old man said cheerfully.

"You say exactly the same thing every week?" I asked.

"Pretty much," he said.

Bessie stabbed her needle into the quilt. "I say he should keep right on saying it till they hear."

"Mrs. Wilson says I'm a broken record," said the old man, not seeming to mind the criticism one bit.

I made a face. "I met *her*."

"Old cow," Bessie agreed.

"Sounding unchristian in there," called Fred from the kitchen.

"Oh, hush up, you old heathen," Bessie said. "We're speaking gospel truths."

"So what is it you're saying over and over?" I asked.

"That we should love God and each other," the Padre replied matter-of-factly. "That's the heart of the matter."

I thought a lot could be said for his message, except the God part.

"Maybe," I ventured, "it's *how* you're saying it. I could help you write it, except . . ."

"Except what?" the Padre asked.

"God's not really my favorite subject."

"What do you mean?" he said.

I hesitated.

"Spit it out," Bessie said. "We speak our minds around here."

"And then some," Fred said, coming back with her tea and several pills on a tray. He set the tray on Bessie's lap with a look of worried adoration.

"Well," I said, "if I ever come face to face with God Almighty, He's got some serious explaining to do. I got a whole list of things to ask Him, starting with why He gave me to the mama He did."

They all three stared at me for a few seconds, but two shakes later you never heard a roomful of people laugh so hard.

"Honey," Bessie said, "you and I are going to be best friends."

"You know," the Padre said, "a story along those lines might be just the thing. A story about Saint Teresa of Avila."

I knew some about saints. Manny's mama, Rita, was a regular churchgoer, and she'd hauled me with her to Sunday Mass sometimes. She talked about Saint This One and Saint That One like they were her next-door neighbors or people she'd just run into at the grocery store, except that they wore halos. "I asked Saint Martha to get Manny Sr. off his lazy butt to help me with the dishes," she'd say, or "I'd still be wandering the mall parking lot if Saint Anthony hadn't helped me find my Eldorado." Rita said every saint had special abilities, like Saint Anthony finding lost things and Saint Martha helping housewives. She herself had been named after Saint Rita, patron saint of the impossible, because the doctor had told Rita's mama that she couldn't have kids. Rita's second favorite was Saint Jude Thaddeus, helper of hopeless causes. Rita was forever burning poor Saint Jude's ear about Manny.

"I've never heard of Saint Teresa," I said.

"You remind me of her," said the Padre.

"How come?"

"About five hundred years ago Saint Teresa was riding through Spain on a donkey. God knocked her off the donkey into the dirt and said, 'That's how I treat My friends.' And she replied, 'That's why You have so few of them.'"

The Padre gave us a sly look and we all laughed.

"Saint Teresa, one," I said, licking my finger and marking an imaginary score in the air. "God, nothing."

"Nice touch," the Padre said.

"That story'd start a fine sermon," I told him, "but Mrs. Wilson won't like it."

"She'll have a fit!" Bessie cried, cackling.

"You be sure and tell her where you got the idea," I said.

"Y'all are piling up serious purgatory time today," Fred teased.

But Bessie just grinned. "Worth every suffering minute."

"I know another story," the Padre said.

"Another saint story?"

He considered. "Could be."

I sat back in my chair.

"It's about the day Henry hung the crucifix Bessie hired him to make in the church," the Padre said. "It was four or five years ago, about an hour before the Saturday vigil Mass. I was in the sacristy, right off the altar. A few members of the parish had come to church early and were kneeling in prayer. Henry was up on a rickety ladder at the back of the altar. The plaster he was trying to drill into was crumbling, and Henry was telling that plaster where it could go and calling upon any number of holy names."

"That's Henry," I said.

The Padre nodded. "This went on for some time. One of the more diplomatic church ladies came to me, all anxious and wringing her hands, and she said, 'Father, Father, you've got to speak to Dr. Royster about his blaspheming! The parishioners are complaining. Please ask him to stop.'

"I said, 'I'm aware of the situation, Abigail, and sympathetic to your discomfort, but I never interrupt a man when he's praying.'"

We all burst out laughing again, Bessie most of all.

"I'll never forget, Lucinda Wilson came in right after Henry finished putting up that cross," the Padre said. "She took one look at it and said to Henry's face, 'That's the ugliest thing I've ever seen.' And Henry told her, 'If you close your eyes, it will go away.'"

Bessie clapped her hands, said she never tired of hearing that story, and demanded another, but Fred told her she needed her afternoon nap. She fussed about that, saying he kept her chained to her bed, but I thought she looked tired.

She seemed to read my mind, because as Fred was helping the Padre rise from his chair, she reached out for my hands again, looked me in the eye, and said, "Don't let Fred turn you into an old mother hen. One's more than enough around here. And tell Henry Royster I said he's the second-sweetest man who ever lived."

Sweet was not a word I associated with Henry, and I swear she saw me thinking that, too, because she squinted and said, "You'll see."

"You a mind reader?" I asked her.

She pressed my cheeks between her cool hands. "Honey," she whispered, "your face is as clear as glass."

I was going to have to watch myself around Bessie.

Fred and I drove the Padre back to his church, which was not far up the road from Henry's. It was a white frame country church with a steeple and a graveyard beside it. A couple of old ladies looked up from arranging flowers in the headstone urns and waved. The Padre shuddered and slid down in his seat. "Hideous," he said, shaking his head. "A slap in the Creator's face."

"What?" I asked.

"Plastic flowers. Abominable things."

This was some strange holy man. "If you close your eyes . . ." I reminded him.

"Quite right," he said, smiling. "Please get me inside so I don't have to look at them."

The church was empty and hushed. He showed me the

crucifix Henry had made for the altar, as unusual a thing as I'd ever seen. It wasn't at all like the crucifixes in Rita's church. It was made with just two pieces of curved silver metal attached to a plain darker metal cross. The Padre pointed out that the lighter silver metal represented Jesus' outstretched arms and twisted body, and that spare as the piece was, it was exactly right. The metal figure seemed to be dying, rising, comforting, and yearning all at the same time.

Loud banging from Henry's workshop interrupted my replay of the afternoon, but I wasn't letting anything spoil it. I'd won a bet, been fingerprinted, helped write a sermon, and met a mind reader, all in one day. If Henry wanted to be an old crank, let him be one. He could close his eyes anytime; I'd go away.

Henry hammered on, but I drifted off. Next thing I knew, a phone was ringing. Somebody had switched off my light, tucked me under the covers, and set my notebook and pencil on the night table beside a glass of water. I slipped out of bed. From the window I saw the light from Henry's bedroom still shining on the lawn below and heard the sound of his sleepy voice upstairs. I climbed the steps and stood in the dark hall, listening.

"I know, Susan, I got your messages. . . . Yes, well, something more urgent came up and your check slipped my mind, I'm sorry. . . . You know, Susan, it's late. It's been a long day and I'm just too tired to go there tonight. How about I concede that I'm a low-down, no-account rat and put the check in the mail tomorrow? How would that be?"

I stepped silently inside the room as he slammed down the phone. He pushed his glasses up on top of his bare head and rubbed the sleep out of his eyes. He was lying on his bed, dressed in a work shirt and jeans, a book facedown on his chest. Folders and papers and the sheaf of phone messages Fred had taken for him littered the bedspread. He looked up and saw me standing there, and set his glasses back on his nose.

"Sorry about the phone," he said.

"So are you?" I asked him.

"What?"

"A low-down, no-account rat."

He snorted. "My ex-wives certainly think so."

"How many wives have you had?"

"Three."

"All three of them divorced you?"

"Just two."

"How come?"

Henry shrugged. "I'm not easy to live with."

"Me either."

"No?"

I shook my head. "Mama said I was the most cussed person she'd ever met."

"Is it true?" he said, turning the tables.

"I've got a temper."

"Welcome to the Royster family."

"Which wife was that on the phone?"

"Number two. Susan. The woman I thought I *ought* to marry. Beautiful, smart, the kind of woman who could take me places. In our case, straight to the devil."

"What happened to number one?" I said.

"Who knows? She took the settlement and ran."

"And number three?"

His voice softened. "Cancer," he whispered, in a subject-closed way.

"I'm sorry." I felt bad for bringing it up. "Any kids?"

"You're the first."

This startled me, and I wasn't sure whether in a good way or not. Henry's kid. I'd have to think on that. I moved closer to see the book he was reading. "What's that about?"

He turned the book around and set it on the edge of the bed so I could see. An old lady, wrinkled as a prune and dressed in black, stared back at me. On the facing page stood a low house on a vast desert. I studied the woman's face: old but strong, with piercing eyes.

"Georgia O'Keeffe," Henry said. "She lived in the New Mexico desert. She had a temper, too."

I turned the pages and saw color pictures of painted deserts, big flowers, churches and animal skulls, and more photographs of her house and the land around it, called Ghost Ranch, the caption said. The landscape was large-minded and peaceful, a place I might like to go.

"I like your room," I said.

"Fred said you looked around."

"He said I was nosy."

"Curiosity is a good thing."

"That's what I said!"

"Fred was teasing you. This is your house now too, Zoë. Make yourself at home. Look at anything you like."

"I can read your books?"

"Of course."

"That's good," I said, looking up, "because I already borrowed one. About a Japanese boy who drew cats."

He thought for a moment, then nodded as if remembering. "A good story," he said. "True."

"It really happened?"

"A different kind of true," he said, pointing to his heart. "True here."

I didn't tell him I hadn't read it yet.

"Books are so much easier than people," he said, taking in all the books around the room.

I'd always thought that, but I didn't know anyone else did.

I reached into my T-shirt pocket, took out the ten and two twenties he'd given me earlier, and set them on the bed. "To help with Mama's bill."

"I don't understand."

"I saw in your checkbook. I know you paid it. Five thousand four hundred and fifty dollars, now five thousand four hundred even. It'll take me a while, but I'll pay you back."

"You *were* nosing around, weren't you?" Henry took the bills, folded them, and reached across to slip them back into my pocket. "Let's just say that paying your mother's bill made me feel better about all those years I didn't know about your father and mother and you, all right?"

"How'd you find out? About me, I mean?"

"A man came here one day and told me. Your mother's friend Ray."

I made a face.

Henry went on. "He knew about your father, Owen, from your mother. She told Ray that you were Owen's child. He figured out the rest and found me himself."

I'd never heard anyone speak my daddy's name. Before today, he was just "your father," "your uncle's half-brother." There weren't even pictures of him that anybody knew of. Hearing his name made him seem, for the first time, like a flesh-and-blood person.

Ray told you all this for nothing? I nearly asked, but I stopped myself. Ray never did anything for free. Instead I asked, "You went to pay the hospital today?"

"Yes, and then to my lawyer's to take care of some paperwork. That's why it took all day."

I thought of all the hospitals Mama had stayed in, all pretty much the same as Rose Hill. Locked doors and windows, halls that smelled like cigarettes or pee, and always somebody screaming. Did anybody get well in those places? I was glad Henry had gone alone. I never wanted to see a place like that again.

"Your mother's affairs were . . ." He seemed to be trying to find a softer word than the one I read in his eyes. "Messy," he said finally.

"I thought . . ."

"What?"

"Nothing." Leaving me hadn't occurred to him. Not today, anyway.

But he knew without my saying it. "I won't abandon you, Zoë, not intentionally. Some of the legal papers I signed today—" He glanced at the clock on his night table. It was after one in the morning. "Some of the legal papers I signed *yesterday* insure that if anything *unintentional* ever happens to me, everything I have belongs to you. Everything. This house, the land, the unsold work. Susan's on the installment plan only as long as I'm alive."

I nodded a little and stared into his tired gray eyes. I wanted to believe him, but I'd believed too many grown-ups' promises, all broken. What grown-ups said and what they actually did never matched or even came close. I tried to be happy for all Henry had done, but I knew he'd change his mind in the end, move on, chump out like all the rest.

"I'm real appreciative for all the money you've paid, everything you've done."

He sighed. "I wasn't asking for gratitude," he said. "I was trying—"

The phone rang like a shrill voice. Anger flared in Henry's eyes, and he seemed to forget I was standing there. He snatched up the receiver and held it away from his ear. A raging female shrieked, *"How dare you hang up on me, you miserable—"* Henry slammed down the phone, wrapped the cord twice around his hand, and yanked that sucker right out of the wall.

Just like that.

I must've looked scared, because he glanced at the severed cord and looked embarrassed. "Sorry about that," he said. "What were we saying?"

"It wasn't important," I said. I headed for the stairs so

my clear-as-glass expression wouldn't show what else I was thinking: That if he'd hung up on her, he might hang up on me. "Night, Uncle Henry."

"Sweet dreams, Zo'."

"Yeah," I whispered. "Sweet as they can be."

4

"Do I get a last request?"

Henry was leaning back in his captain's chair at the dinner table, his feet in the chair beside him, sipping a cup of coffee. "You have to go to school."

I poked at my untouched dinner with a fork and didn't answer. I'd decided on a hunger strike, though Fred had cooked meat loaf, creamed potatoes, and buttered baby peas and I could've eaten every bite.

"Did you hear me?"

"I'm not deaf," I said. "Or dumb."

"No one said you were."

"Then I don't see why I have to go. I tested higher than anybody ever has on those tests. That guidance lady said so. She said I did as well as a high school kid."

"On some parts, not others."

"I never had to go before. I learned fine on my own. I can do that here. You can check me."

"I'm not arguing about this anymore," Henry said. "We each have our work to do. I'm going to my studio every morning, and you're going to school. Even if there's nothing they can teach you, it will be good for you to be with other kids."

"*You* don't spend time with anybody but me and Fred and those stupid sculptures!"

"I don't claim to be a role model. But I'm responsible for you now. And I'll be taking you to school at seven-thirty tomorrow morning."

"You promised you wouldn't leave me!"

"Abandonment and education are not the same thing."

I folded my arms across my chest and narrowed my eyes. "I don't feel good. I feel a fatal and highly contagious disease coming on."

Henry seemed to be expecting this. "*That* I know something about."

He got his medical bag from the top shelf of the hall closet and slipped a thermometer in my 98.6° mouth, took my perfectly normal blood pressure, and checked my angry heartbeat with an ice-cold stethoscope.

"I'll just leave my bag out in case you're not feeling well in the morning," he said, and it took all my willpower not to smack him.

"I have some paperwork to do," he said then, and headed to his study. He left the door open so he could keep tabs on me.

"I'll run off," I whispered when I knew he couldn't hear. "And *you* won't find me."

I stayed in my room while he worked late. Around eleven, I crept downstairs. He was busy at his computer but turned an ear to the creaking stairs. I ran back up, closed my bedroom door, and stewed in my window seat, plotting my escape. I thought of the cat outside in the weeds. He and I both had experience making ourselves scarce. Henry didn't understand who he was dealing with. But he'd soon see.

Henry climbed the stairs near midnight, but he didn't go right to bed. His silhouette stretched black against the light from his windows in the backyard below. His looming shadow gave me the creeps. I imagined myself a condemned prisoner in the Henry Royster Maximum Security Prison, complete with searchlights, sirens, guard towers, and vicious, patrolling dogs. Plus the sheriff had my fingerprints. I was doomed.

Others had tried and failed to make me go to school, starting with Lester when I was six. Fourteen stitches and a perfect, permanent impression of my teeth in his right arm had shown him the error of his thinking. A year and a half later, sixty percent of my track winnings convinced Manny that the school of life was as good as formal education. Charlie liked that I read to his mother, and reasoned that I was learning plenty while I did. After that, none of the others cared if I went to school or spent my mornings reading and writing at home, my afternoons and evenings in the library. They liked having the housework done, and Mama sure wasn't going to do it. They'd all skipped school when they were kids, so why shouldn't I? Heck, most of them didn't even wonder where I was unless dishes piled up in the sink, their underwear drawer went empty, or there wasn't any coffee to ease their morning hangovers.

Henry was different. He had money and brains, in addition to legal papers and a fixed idea that he was responsible for me and in charge. My life savings or a few bite marks were not going to change his mind.

My best hope was that he'd hurry up and fall asleep, and once he had, I'd grease the door hinges with salad oil and slip deep into the woods. But Henry's light stayed on and on. My eyelids grew heavy as stones. I sat up taller in the window seat, jerked myself awake, and pinched my cheeks till they burned. It wasn't any good. Sometime around one-thirty, I fell sound asleep.

It seemed like seconds later when I sat bolt upright in my bed. Henry must've found me in the window seat and put me under the covers. Why couldn't he be like the others? Let me keep up my own schooling? Do as I liked?

My clock said four-thirty. It was still dark out, and Henry's lights were finally off. I dressed quickly in my old clothes. I said good-bye to my room and took a long look at the bookcase Fred had fixed for me, my new outfits still in their bags, and all the books Henry had let me borrow. I'd run off for a day, maybe two, three at the outside, just till he learned he wasn't the boss of me. The others had learned. He'd come around in time, and when he did, I'd come back. I stared up the stairs at the third floor, threw one leg over the banister, and slid sound-lessly down.

I hugged the walls, keeping to the less creaky part of the floor next to the baseboards. Ever so quietly I moved a kitchen chair to stand on, greased the front-door hinges with olive oil, and worked the door open inch by inch till the oil sank in. Then I slipped silently outside.

I stood on the porch for a minute, pleased at my success. The autumn nights had turned cooler, and I shivered a little, missing the warmth of my bed. I walked as far as the crate and saw both of the cat's bowls still full of food and water. I didn't feel him near. I crept toward the weeds, hoping to catch sight of him. But his napping spot was bare, the weeds tamped flat. The big trucks coming and going all week to load Henry's sculptures had likely chased him off, I hoped not for good. Lately he'd let me get closer. If Henry stayed pigheaded about school, the cat and I could live in the woods together, happy, wild, and free.

I followed a faint trail through the blackberry brambles down toward a little footbridge that crossed the creek. Even in the dark I smelled cedar and the musk of dry leaves under my feet. This was how the cat knew the world, what he studied to live and make his way. He didn't need schools or teachers or other cats. He read the wind, took his lessons from the woods, studied the chapters of the moon and stars, needing nobody and nothing, living the life I wanted for myself.

I closed my eyes and took a deep breath of freedom. As I did, something stirred in the woods behind me. I spun around and stared. Not twenty feet ahead, a ghost stood on the creek bridge, staring back at me—at least what seemed like a ghost. There, nearly close enough for me to rush forward and touch her, stood a snow-white deer, slender and small—a yearling, to look at her—with a pink nose, pale eyes, and hooves as gray as ashes.

Either I was seeing things or the moonlight was playing

tricks. It had been a long night and I hadn't had much sleep. But the deer stayed put, taking me in as though I was a vision every bit as strange. Maybe she was a spirit, I thought, the wandering shade of some uneasy soul. Lester had told me ghost stories about the restless roamings of the unquiet dead, what he called haints, eerie stories I'd loved. But as soon as I had that thought, the pale creature shook her head as if she'd heard what I was thinking. She stamped and pawed the bridge planks, four solid hooves knocking against solid wood. Then she lifted her pink nose and sniffed me on the air.

She seemed more curious than afraid, and by the way she kept looking back over her shoulder I gathered she wasn't alone. Her attention was split between me and something else—another animal, I thought. An owl in the woods hooted once, twice, then a third time, and finally the deer turned to the woods and bounded off toward the sound. I took off after her as fast as I could.

I quickly lost sight of her, and followed her sound. Her light running barely stirred the leaves, but I heard the other, heavier animal catching up to her, then both of them running full out ahead of me. I kept my arms raised to push back the branches, but twigs lashed my face and hands and slowed me down. I ran deeper and deeper in, the woods growing denser and darker, the moonlight barely shining through the treetops. The deer and her friend ran like the wind while I stumbled and snagged my sweater on every bramble and branch.

Finally I stopped to listen and didn't hear them at all. For a few minutes I moved ahead toward where I'd last heard them, but it wasn't any good. Either they'd run beyond earshot or they'd stopped to keep their hiding place hidden. They wouldn't be found unless they cared to be. I heard only the wind in the treetops, the far rushing of the stream.

5

The next thing I knew, it was morning. I woke up in my bed, dressed in my escape clothes, without the first idea of how I'd gotten back. I remembered getting lost in Henry's woods, pausing to rest against the trunk of a big tree, and having this weird dream about my daddy. At least I understood him to be my daddy, the way you understand things in dreams. The white deer stood close by looking curious, and Daddy seemed put out with her, I didn't know why. Both of them stood over me for a long time like they were trying to decide what to make of me. Then Daddy carried me back to Henry's, up the stairs to my room.

Maybe a minute after I woke up, Henry was standing over my bed, looking put out himself and sounding all sarcastic, saying he didn't know too many people who slept in their clothes, but it struck him as a fine morning time-saver. Had I eaten my cereal the night before, too, or would I like a bowl before school? Guess he'd been the one to find me in the woods and haul me back.

I kept up my silent protest against education over an oatmeal breakfast and all the way to the Sugar Hill City School's front office, where trouble started right away. According to the scores from tests I'd taken the week before, I was high-school level in reading and writing and fifth-grade level in math. I hated math, so it was amazing I'd done that well—probably thanks to Manny and our time at the track. In spite of my better test scores, though, and despite the guidance counselor's opinion that I'd be happiest in sixth grade, the county had a rule that "all students should be schooled with peers their own age, exceptions made only in rare circumstances." The assistant superintendent, a bored-looking woman who talked like a robot, showed Henry the rule and didn't even look at me. She said because I'd never attended school, I was "deficient in age-appropriate socialization," and she wouldn't recommend any exception in my case. When Henry asked her to rethink her decision, she told me to wait in the hall. I left the door open a crack and heard her say, "Test results can't always be trusted. Most likely, considering Zoë's near-feral upbringing, her higher numbers are a fluke." Not only did she think I was a savage, she thought I'd cheated somehow.

"You know the thing that burns me most about being a kid?" I yelled at Henry when we got in the truck. "The worst thing about being a kid is that people twice my size with half my brains get to run my life."

Henry sighed. "Wait till you start voting."

"What?" I couldn't believe my ears.

"That woman's an idiot," he went on. "I could send you to boarding school if you want."

"What?" I said again.

"There are some fine boarding schools, but nothing decent nearby."

"I just *got* here," I said. "You want to send me away?"

"I do not. It's the last thing on earth I want, and the last thing you need. But I don't like the alternatives, and neither do you."

"I don't get why I have to go to school at all," I whined.

"It's the law, Zo'. Until you're sixteen, you have to go and I have to send you—somewhere."

"You could teach me."

Henry went quiet when I said this. "Zo'," he said finally. "That's not possible right now. For a lot of reasons."

His jaw tightened. If I pushed harder, he might explode again, maybe yank something out of the dashboard or me out of my seat.

I folded my arms over my chest and went stone quiet as we drove. I gave Henry credit for taking my side with the assistant superintendent, but when I got to thinking how I was the one who'd have to sit stupefied for seven hours a day, five days a week, I took my credit back.

The upshot was that I was stuck in fifth grade. My teacher, Ms. Avery, was nice enough but as dull as petunias. Her saving grace was that she repeated every question at least once and prefaced the second or third asking with a specific kid's name. This meant I could spend the day reading books from Henry's library, coming back to reality only when my name was called.

"Class, who remembers the capital of Montana? Anyone? Zoë, do you remember the capital of Montana?"

"Helena, ma'am," I answered.

The lessons were dirt easy and I nearly always knew the answer, though I never offered it unless Ms. Avery called on me. Everybody hated kids who showboated. Ross Purcell raised his hand so often that I named him Mr. Liberty, which made the other kids laugh. When Ms. Avery called on him he had the ugly habit of making a know-it-all face at the Mexican girl who didn't speak English on his right, then smirking at the slow kid on his left, before giving his windbag answer.

Worse than Ross was Hargrove Peters, whose surly self sat more lying down than sitting in the last desk by the door. Though we'd never exchanged one word, he spent half of every school day staring at me in a burning way, like he already hated my guts. The last one out the door at the end of the day and late every morning, he barely answered if Ms. Avery called on him and never raised his hand in class. He just glared at me or wrote in some notebook he slammed shut if anybody walked by.

Shelby, the girl who sat across from me, said that Hargrove's daddy was Sugar Hill's mayor, and that made Hargrove think he was better than other people.

"He sure doesn't like me," I said.

"He doesn't like anybody," she said. "Don't pay him any mind. I don't."

But by midweek his staring was bugging me no end. "Is he still staring?" I asked Shelby.

She glanced back and nodded. "Like a cat at a mouse."

A few minutes later I got up to sharpen my pencils at the back of the room and check out Hargrove without him seeing. He'd have to turn all the way around in his desk to stare at me there. I got a tissue first, from a bookcase by the window, and stood there blowing my nose. It bothered him that I was out of view. When I started back across the rear of the room, he stiffened as I got close, slapped his notebook shut, and fidgeted mightily with his pencil. I stood right behind him sharpening one, two, three pencils, as slowly as I could.

Hargrove was good-looking, but he knew it. His hair was cut short and clean above his collar and ears. His clothes were pricey and pressed. But that notebook he carried was old and dog-eared with bent corners and didn't match the rest of him.

I sauntered by him back to my seat. "He's *still* staring?" I asked Shelby without turning around.

She glanced back and nodded again. "Never seen him this weird before."

I whirled around in my seat and glared, catching him off-guard. He lowered his eyes, but just for a second.

"Is there a problem, Zoë?" Ms. Avery asked.

"No, ma'am," I said, and scowled at Hargrove before I turned back around. "No problem at all."

But that didn't stop him. He stared at me clear through spelling and silent reading. And the next day, and the day after that. I didn't even have to ask Shelby anymore to know when he was doing it. I could feel his eyes boring into me, and by week's end I'd had my fill.

On Friday I packed up early and was the first one out of

class. He was the last one out, as usual. I waited for him just beyond the turn to the main hall and stepped right in front of him as he came around the corner. "What?" I snapped, not three inches from his stunned face.

He tried to go around me, but I blocked his path. His face flushed red, but it hardened, too. He tried to dodge me, but I was quick.

"Quit staring at me," I snapped.

"You're crazy," he said, and then added something under his breath that I didn't hear.

"What was that?" I said.

His eyes met mine. "Just like your mother who offed herself," he said, this time loud and mean, and then pushed past me, bumping me sideways into the wall. He walked out the front door without looking back.

That shook me. I leaned against the wall for a minute. I didn't think anybody knew about Mama but me and Henry, and maybe Fred and Bessie, who sure wouldn't say anything to Hargrove Peters. Mama hadn't been my favorite person, but I didn't like some uppity loser kid, who didn't know us from dirt, talking about her like that. I didn't like it one bit.

The principal, Mr. Reardon, was coming down the hall. He stank of the cigarettes he sneaked in the janitor's closet, and had a seen-it-all, heard-it-all, done-it-all attitude toward kid behavior. He ran the school with horse sense and humor dry as dust. I liked him, and I could tell he liked me back.

"What's shaking, kiddo?" he said, smiling. "How's the world treating you?"

"Fine," I lied. "Fine as can be." Which is what I said to Fred when he picked me up outside, and to Henry when he asked at dinner how school was going.

After that, only one thing made school bearable: Ms. Avery wasn't as dull as I'd thought. When I got to my desk on Monday, I found a book and a note: *I think you might like this, if you haven't already read it. If you like it, I have others. E. Avery.* It was called *They Came Like Swallows* by William Maxwell. I'd never read it. I started it right then and lapped it up—about eight-year-old Peter, called Bunny, his thirteen-year-old brother, Robert, their daddy, James, and their mama, who died of the influenza. I read the whole book in one day.

I lived for Ms. Avery's books and for the last bell, when Henry or Fred picked me up and drove me back to the house. Except for Hargrove, my classmates were nice enough but boring—they automatically did whatever the nearest grown-up expected. I was nice back, but that was all. When Henry or Fred asked about my day, I kept quiet. If fifth grade was crammed down my throat, I wasn't going to waste time puking it back up.

Henry took my attitude in stride. "It's how I'd feel," I over-heard him tell Fred, after which he added that between paying alimony, Mama's debts, and his lawyer, he was pretty strapped for cash and needed to get into the studio and stay there if we all wanted to eat. For a few hours I felt bad for shutting him out, but my heart rehardened against him when I saw Hargrove at school the next day. Henry had till Christmas. Then we'd see.

When summer turned to autumn and trucks thundered night and day up and down the man's drive, he changed his mind again about humans. The whole species was a restless, sleepless, earsplitting scourge upon the earth.

What had come over the place? Dog or no, the man had once seemed to know about solitude, the space a creature needed. Now, morning till night, men swarmed the place like ants, hauling off the metal things the man made. They wrenched them apart, lifted and lowered the separate pieces with roaring machines, shouted and cursed as they lashed and bound the pieces with ropes. Then the trucks rumbled off, raising clouds of dust. The cat sneezed and shook his head, fled under the house to ease the buzzing in his ears, the pounding in his head.

After that the boy came. The boy who used to mind his own business. Who'd gone and stayed gone for whole seasons, kept to his own turf. Even *he* traipsed right through the yard with his dimwitted deer, carried the sleeping girl straight up the front steps, through the front door and inside the house. Had they all gone mad?

The girl disappointed him most. Kindred at first, she'd lingered after she filled his bowls, sat for hours near the weeds and whispered to him, her voice soothing and sweet. He had liked having her near. She'd stretched on the grass, pretending to read, stare at the sky, watch clouds, all the while inching closer when she thought he didn't see.

Then she and the man had argued, and the girl must have lost. He'd watched her run off, the boy bring her back. Since then, she left early, returned late, tore off into the woods till dark, and seemed to have forgotten all about him.

It was all too much. He shunned the food in his bowls, took to the woods beyond the stone garden, and made for the steepled house to hunt rats.

He slept under the white wooden building, near the larger stone garden there. Sometimes bells rang in the steeple, or people strolled in the garden or gathered in the building overhead, but for several days the place had been quiet. He napped and hunted, hunted and napped.

Hungry now, he stared out at the stones, watched and listened for dart or scurry. He'd stopped thinking the human habit of stone-planting peculiar. He saw the uses in it now. The flat stones were good for sleeping on, cool in summer and toasty in winter when the sun warmed them. The upright

ones broke the wind and kept off the rain and snow if he stayed to the lee side. Best of all, the stone garden earth teemed with fat brown rats, his favorite meal.

The strange objects planted in front of the stones puzzled him, though. They had no use that he could find. They looked like flowers, but weren't flowers. He sniffed them, but they had no smell. He bit them, but they had no taste. They weren't cold or warm. They didn't rot or die. They stood mute, stiff, the same in every season, without growth or new blossom. Even the rats, who ate garbage, shunned them.

One afternoon an old woman had caught him peeing on the largest bunch. She chased him into the crawlspace, screeching at him and waving her arms. From his hiding place he saw her pluck the dripping objects out of  the ground with her thumb and forefinger, wash off his scent under a nearby spigot, and then replant them, grumbling all the while. After that, he supposed the objects marked territories, something he understood, and he peed on them whenever possible, the old woman's bunch doubly, though he waited in vain for her to do the same.

Suddenly he heard doors slamming outside, footsteps on the

front walk, the whoosh of the entry door, then hushed human voices overhead. The footsteps and voices upstairs grew closer and echoed in the large space. He heard women's and men's voices both, one he recognized: the voice of the woman who'd screamed at him, as usual screeching about something.

He's under there, all right, she said. I saw him go through the vent. He does his business on Harold's grave and I won't have it. I say put down poison and be done with him.

Whose cat is he? said a man. Does he belong to someone? The cat knew this voice, too. It belonged to the hobbling, white-haired old man with the cane who stood before the townspeople when they gathered upstairs, speaking to them in earnest tones.

Don't know, Father, said a second man. He don't act domesticated, but he's one heck of a ratter. He's doing you a favor.

Favor! cried the woman.

It's the God's truth, Constance, said the old man. The rats are bad this year. Answer to a prayer, I'd say.

Father, you're not suggesting that God sent that cat to urinate on my Harold's grave? asked the woman, incredulous.

The Lord's ways are mysterious, said the old man. We're simply saying that the up side might be more important than the down side.

Unless Harold's fond of rats, said the second man.

I can't see poisoning God's creature for the sake of plastic flowers, the old man said. What if he belongs to someone? Dr. Royster's isn't far.

Tomcats run in that family, said the woman.

What if Mr. Pendergrass hoses off your flowers once a week,

Constance? said the old man, exasperated. Would that do?

For a few moments there was silence.

I suppose, said the woman tightly. For now. But if it doesn't . . .

Faith, Constance, and enjoy your organ practice, the old man said.

The men left then. But the woman stayed and stomp-stomp-stomped up the back stairs and across the upper floor, grumbling and sniping. All at once a horrid noise boomed and blared overhead, shaking the walls and thundering through the ductwork as the woman caterwauled along. The cat shot out of the crawlspace into the woods, his head pounding, and wished they would all shut up.

6

The minute I got home from school every day, I headed for the woods, listening and searching for any sign of the white deer and her friend. In two weeks' time I'd explored the woods to the east, south, and west, finding nothing but trees. North was what remained.

I headed that way on a cool, bright Friday afternoon, figuring if I didn't find anything by sundown I'd have the weekend to widen my search. It was barely October, but this year's Indian summer had ended early, and a chill had settled in the air. Winter was coming soon.

I looked for the cat as I went. I hadn't seen much of him since school started, and the trucks had kept coming and going, delivering Henry's supplies and taking finished sculptures away. The food in his bowls was nibbled some days, untouched others. I hoped he was okay.

Henry's property ended near what Fred called the "old growth," and I thought these northernmost woods were what he meant. The trees were bigger and older here, some as big around as truck tires. That made walking easier, since not much grew in their deep shade. Fallen branches rotted in loose heaps in the leaf litter, but the piles had an order that I doubted nature had made by herself. These older woods seemed tended, even loved.

I was about to head back near sunset when I heard rustling to my right and turned to see the white deer above me on the rise, her pink nose raised in greeting. She kept more distance this time, about twenty yards, though she didn't look afraid. I stood perfectly still, not wanting to spook her. Her ears twitched and swiveled, scanning the woods for sounds. She kept looking over her shoulder, and I understood the presence of her companion, though I saw or heard no other sign of him.

Once again an owl hooted insistently from the trees. The deer turned slightly in the call's direction. When the owl hooted a second time, and louder and more urgently a third, the deer looked back at me as if to apologize, then reluctantly cantered off into the trees toward the mournful sound.

I wasn't fool enough to try to catch her this time, but I hurried on in that direction and kept her in sight as long as I could. A half-mile or so on, something silver glinted from behind a stand of trees. As I got closer, I saw an old trailer shaped like a big silver bullet. I knocked, but nobody answered, so I peered inside. It was filthy and full of old spider webs, pine needles, and dry leaves, but otherwise it was completely empty; not a dish on the dusty kitchen counters or shelves, no cushions in the seats in what passed for a living room, no curtains in the windows, and not so much as a pencil on the dinette to the right of the door. I saw no road or path outside, and thought the trailer must have been towed here, through a leaner forest years before. But nobody had lived in it for a long time.

I squinted past the trailer. A break of slender pines formed a kind of screen, and beyond that was the roofline of a house. When I came around the trees to look, I found a log cabin. The walls were made of big notched logs, the roof of silver-gray shingles. At one end of the cabin was a stone chimney, and across the front was a porch just big enough for two broken chairs and a rusty motorcycle missing a back tire.

The frame of the cabin looked old, but other parts seemed newer and built in unusual ways. The window frames were made of odd pieces of different kinds of wood, whittled and joined like a puzzle. The window dividers were all sizes and shapes, custom-carved to fit the frames, and broken pieces of clear and colored glass made up the panes. These pieces had been glued or taped together, and set into the frames like a see-through mosaic.

Out front was a covered stone well with a roped bucket for drawing water. To one side, a couple of pumpkins rotted in an old fenced-in garden, and to the other I saw a woodpile and an ax rusting in an old stump.

It didn't look like anyone lived there now. The front door stood ajar, and I invited myself inside.

If people had lived here, they'd lived hard. The single, good-sized room was covered in dust, cobwebs, tracked-in dirt, and leaves. The seat cushions from the trailer made up the mattress of a corner pallet bed heaped with old blankets, brown-stained pillows without cases, and faded quilts that sent up a cloud of dust when I sat down. In the center of the room, a table made from an old door with two tree stumps for legs was covered with broken strands of fishing line, jaybird feathers for lures, and pebbles for sinkers. A pair of plain stools stood beside it, one tall and one kid-sized. Two dusty oil lamps sat on the wide mantel above the hearth, and in the fireplace an old oven rack spanned red bricks stacked four high on either side. The ashes were clumped and cold. On the back wall to the right were some open shelves holding a few dented pots and utensils, and below that was a stone sink with no tap. Whoever had lived here had hauled water from the well to drink and wash.

Along the walls, crude shelves overflowed with natural trea-sures, things a kid might keep. Crow, bluebird, and cardinal feathers and a single peacock plume lay alongside other feathers I didn't know on one shelf. Another was crowded with large and small birds' nests and eggs that hadn't hatched—blue, green, pink, and speckled—next to a much larger collection of broken shells. Other shelves held the gray-striped papery makings from a wasp's nest, animal bones, and small skulls bleached white by the sun, like little versions of those in Ms. O'Keeffe's pictures. Pinecones the size of pineapples sat next to a dozen tiny ones no bigger than thimbles. There were twigs overgrown with gray, blue, and green lichens, and dozens of rocks, stones, and pebbles polished smooth.

I took down a few of the treasures from the shelves and sat on the bed to study them: a big turtle shell, a coppery striped snakeskin, a perfect arrowhead, and a tiny bird's nest no bigger than a plum half with the pit gone. Underneath the quilts, at the head of the bed, I felt something four-cornered and hard. I pulled back the covers and found an old cigar box. I lifted the lid. On top was a worn black-and-white photograph of a homely-looking woman. She seemed surprised by the camera. Her hair was tied up in bun, with wispy strands escaping every which way. Her dark eyes seemed sad. On the back, a child's hand had scrawled one word: *Mama.*

I lifted her picture to see what lay underneath. A miniature wooden menagerie stared up at me. Half a dozen small animals, carved in wood, were nestled in a bed of dry leaves. A squirrel no bigger than my thumb stood up on its hind legs with a perfect miniature acorn in its paws. A field mouse nibbled a single kernel of corn with tiny teeth. A mama possum nursed her three babies. A raccoon sat on its back legs and washed its bandit face with its paws. An otter floated happily on its back in a pool of water. And the last was a sleeping doe exactly like the white deer. Each one was the spitting image of the living animal, down to the smallest ear, tooth, or claw. Each was satiny smooth and polished to a soft shine.

I marveled at each one and then set them carefully in the box just like I'd found them. I shut the lid and put the box back under the quilt. Surely no one would have left such treasures behind unless they had to. Not unless something sudden or terrible had happened.

I felt uneasy then. The light was fading fast outside, the sun going down. Once it got dark, I might not find my way back.

Before I left, I made sure everything was the way I'd found it. I knew I'd be back soon.

In years past, he'd sensed bad weather before it came: rain in the heft of the air, ice and snow in the steely grayness of the light. Not this time.

This year it snowed impossibly early, in flurries at first, then thickly in large, wet flakes. The wind cut easily through his coat and chilled his old bones. His head, his ears, his eyes, his whole aching body told him that winter had come, and that this winter might be his last.

He found his bowls full and waiting for him in the crate at the edge of the man's front yard. He ate gratefully. The trucks were gone for now, the house dark and quiet. He curled up in the crawlspace, next to the furnace, to get some sleep.

In the morning, he stared out the crawlspace opening at the white world. A foot of snow had swept in as he slept, blanketed his bowls, buried his crate, drifted to cover the crawlspace opening except for a band of daylight at the top. So what? It was warm near the furnace. He had eaten the night before. Water was everywhere. So it was frozen. It would melt.

The snow surprised the girl, too. He heard her shriek overhead in wonder and race outside, heard the door slam behind her. She shouted in delight. No school! No school! Uncle Henry! Come see!

The cat left his place by the furnace, peered through a crack high in the foundation.

The man stormed sleepily after her. Put some clothes on! Shoes at least! For God's sake, are you crazy?

Oh yes! Oh yes yes yes! she cried, throwing armfuls of powder in the air. What will the crazy girl do first? Throw snowballs? Kerpow!

Hey! the man shouted as one hit him. Hey now! But she didn't stop, and they erupted into a squealing, shouting duet, a snowy commotion of man and girl.

The cat watched the girl go wild and hurl snowballs at the man, his arms crossed in front of his face. Zing! Splat! she taunted as snowballs flew and landed, sailed and missed.

The man rushed her then, lunged, caught her around the waist, scooped her up in his arms, and swept her onto the porch.

Put me down! she cried. No fair!

She kicked and screamed an empty kind of scream, like when the cat's stomach was full and he toyed with his food. The girl could easily have kicked harder, bit or scratched the man if she wanted to, wriggled free, and the man held her loosely, his anger a sham. Both were red, wet, shivering, bickering without meaning it. The man whisked her inside because she let him, because she wanted him to.

What would that be like?

7

Snow! In October! The second I saw it I raced outside in my bathrobe, with killjoy Henry hard behind me, calling me crazy. I got even, though. I hurled snowballs at him till he wore snow from head to toe, before he finally bulled his way to me, picked me up, and hauled me back inside.

He brushed off his snow coat and frowned at me, shaking his head. "Hot shower, warm clothes," he said, pointing up the stairs.

By the time I came back down, he'd made hot chocolate, lit a fire in the study fireplace, and moved two easy chairs in front of the hearth with the ottoman between them. He was settled in the far chair, sipping his cocoa. His face was still splotchy from the cold and he was rubbing his bare head, which he did absentmindedly when he was thinking. He crossed his long legs on the ottoman and wriggled his bare toes.

I sat in the other chair, cupped my hands around the steaming mug, and stretched out my own legs beside his. His feet were just like mine, only bigger, the toes long, the second toes longer than the others and rounded at the top. "We have the same feet," I said, turning mine in the warmth. "Only mine are small."

He nodded like he already knew. "One of many things we have in common."

I looked at him. "Oh, yeah? What else?"

I waited while he considered. I was no end pleased I wouldn't be sitting in school today with Hargrove Peters staring a hole in the back of my head. My mind wandered to the cabin in the woods, and I wished I could go see it in the snow. Then I heard a faint mew under the house. I closed my eyes to listen and heard it again. The cat was safe and close by and sleeping somewhere warm.

"We're impulsive," Henry said finally.

"What?" I snapped, my happy thoughts interrupted.

Henry turned back to the fire. "And short-tempered."

"What are you talking about?" I said irritably.

"Nothing."

"I just heard the cat," I said in a nicer voice. "He's under the house."

He turned back to me. "I didn't hear anything."

You wouldn't, I thought, but I didn't say it. "What else?"

"Else?"

"You said we had lots in common."

He lifted his eyebrows and looked at me over his glasses. "We're moody."

"Who!"

"Both of us."

"Speak for yourself!" I snapped again. "I just think deep. That's different."

"If you say so," Henry said.

"*Mama* was moody," I said, stung. It hurt being called something she was. Like being called crazy. *Again.*

Henry nodded. "My mother was that way too."

"You mean crazy?" I blurted before I thought.

"I'm sorry I said that, Zo'," Henry said gently. "I didn't mean it like that."

He leaned forward, set his mug down on the hearth, and stretched to take a leather-bound album from the bookcase. He wiped the dust off the cover with his forearm. The spine crackled as he opened it. He set it on the chair arms between us. Yellowed black-and-white photographs were glued to the pages or stuck loose in between. In one, a stringy, sour-faced man stood impatiently in front of Henry's house. He looked like he wanted to strangle the photographer.

"Who's that?" I asked, pointing.

"*That* is the sole surviving photograph of Edward Augustus Royster, my father, your grandfather."

"He doesn't look happy."

"Happiness wasn't something he valued or sought."

"What did he prize?"

"Hard work. Discipline. Facts he could prove. He analyzed soil samples for the county."

He pointed to another picture, one of a frail, needy-looking woman. She was clutching the collar of her housedress to her throat and staring out as though something scary was about to happen.

"Who's that?" I asked.

"My mother."

"What was she like?"

"Like your mother in her own way."

I chose my words carefully. "Sick in her mind?"

"Yes."

"What else was she like?"

He pondered the question. "I really don't have the first idea what she was like under all that illness."

I studied Henry for signs that he might be making this up, but his expression was matter-of-fact. I knew exactly what he meant. I'd known Mama's sickness, but I didn't know her. I knew her up times when she'd go out and buy things we couldn't afford or get all made up and go out to bars to meet men. I knew her down times when she barely talked and shut herself in her room for days or even weeks. Her drugged times when she was woozy and confused. And the times she was trying to quit, when she'd be sickly sweet one minute, mean and spiteful the next. From one hour to another, I never knew what kind of mood she'd be in. I'd learned early to keep to myself, stay clear. My happiest times had been when Mama was in the hospital.

"Did you love your mama?" I asked Henry.

He thought for a long minute. "If I did, I don't remember."

"I don't remember either," I said, feeling uneasy. "I felt for Mama in my way. When I was real little, I thought she couldn't help being sick. But as I got older I saw she *could* help it some of the time. She'd flat ignore the doctors and do as she liked. They'd say, 'Take your medicine every day, and don't take too much or drink alcohol.' But she heard and did what she wanted to, over and over again.

"She kept bringing home one man after another, even though they all left once they figured her out. She never could keep a job, because when she didn't feel like working she'd find a reason not to show up. We were always owing money and moving because of it. When we had a phone, it rang all day with people trying to collect. She'd say, 'Baby, I'm doing the best I can,' like I didn't have eyes in my head, like I couldn't see how she did exactly as she pleased, the heck with everybody else."

I suddenly felt like I'd said more than I should. But Henry was just listening and nodding, like we were having any old conversation, like he knew.

"But I don't remember loving Mama," I said. "I worry about that sometimes."

"Why?"

"You know how people are."

"What people?"

Everybody, Hargrove, you, I thought, but didn't say. "You know, like that lady in the supermarket? The nosy one? People who like to say what you are, when they don't even know you, and how you *ought* to be and feel."

Henry scowled. "I don't give a flying flip what Lucinda Wilson thinks, and neither should you. You're smarter than that. Another thing we share."

"But you—"

"Wanted to get away from her as fast as possible."

I stared at him, open-mouthed. So *that's* why he'd told me to zip it. "What happened to your mama?" I asked.

"Her heart gave out, like your friend Mrs. King's."

He remembered. "When you were a kid?" I asked.

He shook his head. "Later, when I was grown and as far away from here as I could get. I left home feeling exactly the way you described."

"Really?"

He nodded.

"You were angry?"

"Oh, yes," he said, like any sane person would be crazy not to be.

"Do you still feel like that?"

"Sure."

"Is that why you curse so much?"

He laughed a little. "Metal is a cursed medium."

We both turned back to the fire then and sat staring at the flames and watching the snowfall while we finished our cocoa. I was turning over in my mind all we'd said about our crazy mamas when suddenly Henry broke the spell, tossed the picture album down with a loud slap, and stood up.

"I think I'll go out to the studio for a while," he said, and just as I was thinking he'd had enough of me, he added, "Want to come?"

Henry rolled aside the two-story sliding doors to his workshop, and I walked into a space as big as a warehouse. A wonderful warehouse.

While Henry lit his heaters, I wandered around. Everywhere I looked I saw metal, metal of every size, shape, and kind. Shiny and rusty metal, solid and hollow metal, and metal in chunks, lengths, and sheets. Metal shafts, pipes, and rods; metal gears and cogs; metal circles, triangles, rectangles, spirals, and squares. Metal was leaned, heaped, and hung along every wall. It sagged every shelf, and cluttered every bench, table, and chair. It spanned the steel ribs of the ceiling, dangled from overhead chains. Scraps of it littered the concrete floor like rusty confetti.

Henry wasn't tidy. Hammers, screwdrivers, mallets, chisels, clamps, and files lay scattered where their usefulness had ended. Orange, yellow, and black electric cords stretched and coiled across the ceiling and floor, carrying power to Henry's welders, grinders, saws, work lights, and drills. There were ladders, short, medium, and tall, big fans for ventilation, and motorized hooks for hoisting the heaviest pieces and moving them through the air.

I knew something about machines and tools from waiting for Harlan to quit work at the gas station, and from hanging around the piddling worktables Mama's friends had set up when they moved in. But this was no two-bit service bay or basement hobby shop; this was an honest-to-God workshop, where Henry worked from morning till night.

A large, unfinished piece that looked like an armored elephant filled one corner of the studio. It wore a coppery turban that whirled in the slightest wind.

"Is that what you're working on?" I asked him.

"One of the things," he said.

"Where'd you get all the metal?"

"Scrapyards, mostly. Places that sell all kinds of used metal, acres and acres of it. I take my truck and trailer and see what interests me. A lot of it doesn't look like much when I first bring it back. See these?" He pointed to a stack of double-decker metal rounds about as big around as dinner plates. "These are old disc brakes."

"Car brakes?"

"Yep. They make nice bases for sculptures. And these," he said, picking up two smaller rounds with metal teeth around the outside, "these are sprockets, and this"—he took up a rusty four-pronged thing—"what would you say this was?"

"A pitchfork?"

"Exactly so," he said, pleased. He carefully picked up a long sharp-edged rectangle with a hole dead center. "And this?"

I studied it. "Give me a hint."

"Your mother's friend Charlie would know this," he said.

"A lawnmower blade!" I said. "I saw him sharpen one of those once. Using . . ." I looked around for the tool I wanted, and spied the grinding wheels on top of a red stand. "That!"

"A grinder. You've been paying attention," he said.

Henry didn't talk down to me the way Mama's friends sometimes had. He showed me the differences between the metals: reddish copper, blackish cast iron ("Cursed brittle," he said), silvery aluminum, dull carbon steel, and its shinier stainless-steel cousin. He explained that he joined metal by welding, and that the other tools in his shop were used to cut, shape, finish, or move the welded work.

He chose a length of silver metal about twenty feet long and maybe three inches wide from a stack leaning against the wall.

"Watch," he said. "See how this is square on the outside and hollow on the inside?" He slipped on a pair of work gloves. "I'm going to put it through the bender to round the metal into a big circle."

The bender looked like a big parking meter with a captain's wheel attached to the front. Henry worked fast. He fed one end of the tubing into the bender's left side, then turned the wheel till it came out curved on the right. After that, he took up his welding helmet and handed me one too. He turned a valve on a tank that looked like a scuba diver's and told me how heat, wire, and gas all worked together to make the silvery welds that fused the pieces of metal.

"Like metal glue," I said.

"Welds are stronger than glue, as strong as the metal itself. Welds bind the steel of skyscrapers and bridges together. A good weld almost never breaks."

I thought of Bessie. Too bad a strong weld couldn't fix her heart.

Henry showed me how to put on my helmet, and with the flip of a switch his welder whirred to life. It was dusty and dark inside the helmet, my breathing loud and strange, and I could barely see through the little window in front. Henry pointed the torch tip where he wanted to weld the two ends of the tubing together to close his circle. His torch crackled and burned a bright, eerie green, shooting sparks like a huge Independence

Day sparkler. It was winter and snowing outside, but inside it was the Fourth of July.

My mind eased as I watched Henry work. Our conversation about craziness seemed a long time ago. Henry turned on his grinder to smooth out the welds, making his circle one seamless round. Working calmed Henry, and smoothed out his rough edges too. He took up another piece of tubing and then another, turning them into perfect circles like the first.

I tried to ask more questions, but he was concentrating hard and his machines drowned out talk. That was the way he liked it, I thought. Other people weren't his thing. His conversation was with whatever he was making. We were only a few feet apart, but he got more distant by the minute, till he was in another place entirely, a world he'd escaped to, population one.

8

Henry's admirers were always stopping by, people who'd heard about his work and wanted to meet him in person. Other folks came to hire Henry to make something special. A commission, Henry called it. Sometimes the local farmers brought their broken tractors for Henry to weld, which he did, every bit as carefully as he welded his sculptures. Visitors wandered around and looked at the pieces in the yard, and if Henry's studio door was open, they might duck in to say hey. Now and then someone came to buy one of the sculptures in the yard, or, as Henry called it, "give a sculpture a job."

When I saw the old lady park her pickup in the drive, get out, and take a long look around, I guessed she'd come to browse or have some welding done. Fred was buying groceries and Henry had gone up the road to look in on Bessie. The snow'd finally melted enough for easy walking in the woods, and I was itching to get to the cabin. Henry and I were getting along better since the storm, but he'd been working day and night ever since, occasionally sleeping in his studio. School aside, it wasn't a rotten life, but sometimes Henry was as absent as

Mama, reminding me that people and situations could change. Any thinking orphan had a fallback plan. The empty cabin in Henry's north woods was mine.

"Well, if it's not the wild child," the woman said the second I answered her knock. Her old eyes fixed on me, and starting at the top of my head, she studied every inch, giving me as close an inspection as I've ever had. I swore she counted I had ten fingers and ten toes and everything else besides.

"Beg pardon, ma'am?"

"It's what the whole county's saying. Thought I'd see for myself," she said, and went on studying me from the other side of the screen. I studied her back. She was bundled against the cold; her coarse gray hair was pulled tightly into a bun at the back of her head. She was stringy, her face leathery, her old-lady eyes as penetrating as Ms. O'Keeffe's.

"Uncle Henry's gone out for a while," I told her. "He shouldn't be too much longer, if you'd like to leave word."

"I didn't come to see Dr. Royster," she said. "Step out here where I can see you."

She didn't look dangerous, so I did.

"Nothing the least bit wild about you," the woman said, shaking her head. "Small minds and wagging tongues, should've known."

"Ma'am?"

"Though wagging tongues *can* serve a useful purpose. I've been grateful for the rumors that Roysters and Bookers shoot hunters trespassing on their land."

"Yes, ma'am," I said, remembering Ray. He *liked* to kill living things—squirrels, rabbits, deer—and he wasn't too particular whose land he did it on. I was glad he wasn't anywhere close by. The white deer wouldn't stand a chance.

"He yours?" she said, nodding at the cat. Since the snow he'd taken to lazing in plain sight near his crate at the edge of the yard.

"He's his own cat. But I'm working on him."

"That left ear looks swollen."

"It's been that way for a while."

"Does it stink?"

"Can't get close enough to him to know," I said.

"If it's infected, it could kill him, especially considering how old he looks."

"He won't let anybody near him. Not yet."

"The wild ones are like that," she said, shaking her head. "Once they get a fear of people, it's hard to talk them out of it. I've got a soft spot for old toms. Maud Booker, by the way. I'm the veterinarian around here. My land joins Dr. Royster's about two miles north of here."

She held out her hand and I shook it. Her handshake was like she was, cool and firm.

"Pleased to meet you, ma'am," I said, not sure if I meant it. At least she had good taste in cats.

"I've seen what I needed to see," she said, turning to go. "I never mind other people's business if I can help it. Just wanted to make sure you were all right."

She walked out to her truck, opened the door, and took a small box from a cooler on the back seat. She handed it to me with four cans of cat food. "Fill the little bottle inside the box with water, shake it, and give him a dropperful twice a day in a little of this wet food till it's all gone. If he tames, call me and I'll come give him his shots. I'm in the book."

"Thanks," I said, setting the cans on the ground. I opened the little green box and took out the dropper bottle with white powder inside.

She climbed behind the wheel. "You favor your grandfather."

"I do?"

"You have his chin."

"You knew my grandfather?" I said.

"I knew Augustus well."

"Did you know my daddy?"

"A short while."

"When?"

She started the engine and jerked the pickup into gear. "For the nine months before I gave birth to him."

And she slammed the door and drove off before I could say another word.

He watched her climb the snowy hill and started to follow, until he saw where she was going.

Though it had been years since he'd prowled the north woods, his memory of them was still strong. After she disappeared over the rise, he waited a short while in the cold, then turned back toward the crawlspace under the man's house where it was warm.

When he was a kitten, he'd hunted the woods for rabbits. He missed those days, the time before the savage and his woman had roared up on their sputtering two-wheeled machine and moved into the silver house. The savage had spent his days motoring back and forth between the house and the highway and tending a rattling apparatus he built farther up in the woods. He sang loudly as he worked. Between songs he drank from a jar, and then he went back to tinkering and feeding the fire under his contraption. It was odd-looking, with coils spiraling out of it, smoke and steam escaping in clouds.

While the savage was away, the woman cleaned and swept the silver house. She left bread crusts for the birds and scraps of meat or fish for the cat. Her arms and legs were as fragile as a fawn's, but when her belly grew over the summer, her graceful walk became a waddle. As big as she was, she worked hard. She sloshed bucket after bucket of water from the well into the house, then dragged a heavy basket to a rope strung between trees and hung wet things out to dry. She rarely spoke. The more her stomach grew, the less the man returned to her, though she sat evenings in the doorway as if waiting for him to come. Sometimes she sang in a soft, high voice.

When the savage did come back, he staggered about the yard. He teased the woman, talked loudly, danced her roughly around. Then he slumped to the ground and fell asleep as though dead. The woman covered him with a blanket where he fell. The next morning he seemed a different man. He brought the woman food and drink, laughed nervously as he helped her haul water, hang wash on the line. He put his arms around her, laughing and joking, tipping her chin to make her look at him, listen. She answered with nods, little shakes of her head, and sometimes a frightened smile.

The night the boy was born, the man was out of earshot, snoring beside his contraption. The woman cried out and tumbled down the steps, holding her belly. She writhed for hours in

the dirt, straining, panting, rolling from side to side, calling out, but no one came. The boy slid from between her legs near dawn. He came feet first, covered in blood, and screaming at the top of his tiny lungs. The woman gasped, then lay completely still, her eyes open wide. The boy kicked the air, balled his bloody fists, and wailed.

At sunrise, the savage came. His face was swollen with sleep. He took in the scene as though dreaming. He knelt beside what was left of his family and wept in a raw baritone to the boy's piercing cries. He cradled the inconsolable noise in the crook of his elbow, sliced the cord connecting him to his mother, and shut her staring eyes.

9

The minute the old woman claiming to be my grandmother had gone, I slipped my books into my backpack and headed over the bridge into the north woods.

I didn't know what to think about her claim. The social worker had told Henry and me what she could about my daddy's life. He'd been given up at birth by his unwed mother (Maud Booker, if you believed her), taken in by the Baptist Home, and put up for adoption. His adoption had seemed sure until doctors discovered a defect in his heart. Nobody had wanted a sick baby. So Daddy had grown up with the Baptists till he ran off at fifteen. After that he stole things and was in and out of trouble, till he was killed one night walking on a nearby road, a hit-and-run.

That was all I knew, except that he'd hooked up with Mama long enough to make me, and that he'd lain dead next to Mama longer than he ever had in life.

If Maud Booker had told the truth, she hadn't mothered him long. I wondered if she regretted giving him up, if that was why she'd stopped by. But even if running hunters off her land and giving me medicine for the cat spoke in her favor, I couldn't decide if I wanted to know her better or not. I'd keep her visit to myself until I made up my mind.

As October gave over to November, the woods and cabin became my favorite place to think. I'd given in to Henry about school, but that settled, he pretty much left me to myself. Aloneness was as much his way as mine. I doubted that Henry would have known what to do with me if I'd been a clingy child in need of entertaining—maybe bought a big TV and a DVD player and set me in front of it while he worked. Solitary work was plainly as vital to him as breathing, like reading and writing were to me.

We mostly ate dinner together. Usually it was just Henry and me, a you-read-your-book-and-I'll-read-mine kind of thing, Henry's mind still in his studio and mine with the cat or at the cabin. Now and then Fred and Bessie joined us. One night Fred argued with Henry and Bessie about me running wild. He said I was too young to be roaming the woods alone. Bessie called Fred an old woman, said she'd give anything to be able to run free herself, and threatened to do it one day when Fred wasn't looking. Bessie and Henry said they'd wandered the woods when they were younger than I was. Fred lost, outnumbered. All Henry asked was that I stay on his posted land, wear bright colors against straying hunters, and be home by dark. I promised I would.

So after school on weekdays and after a quick breakfast on weekends, I headed into the woods, the cat not far behind. He started trailing me once Ms. Booker's medicine shrunk the swelling in his ear. He kept his distance—left himself plenty of room to bolt—but stuck close enough to keep me in sight. He hadn't let me touch him yet, but he seemed to be considering it. Every morning I found him waiting for me and his breakfast in the front yard. At night he headed under the house for warmth, but not before sitting for a long time alone in the yard, watching my window. I made him a soft bed by the furnace from an old feather pillow and a blanket and put my stuffed bunny down there so he'd get used to my scent.

Halfway to the cabin, though, was as far as he'd go. His fear of the north woods was powerful, and he flat refused to follow me past the old-growth trees. He'd shadow me over the bridge and partway up the path, then stop cold, turn around, and go back. He turned back in practically the same spot every day, like there was an invisible wall he couldn't go past. I tried to coax him on with a trail of leftovers, but he was stubborn. Something up there scared him, maybe a memory of whoever had lived in the cabin before. I went on without him, but I stayed alert.

I kept a lookout for the white deer, too, but saw no sign of her, though birds and squirrels and other creatures flitted or rustled in the trees. I hoped she and her friend were nearby, watching, and might show themselves soon.

For weeks I cleaned the little cabin and worked to make it tight. I couldn't get much done in the two hours between school and dark, but I made good headway on weekends, sweeping, dusting, and scrubbing till I was sore.

I used old newspapers and a screwdriver to chink the drafty

open places between the cabin logs. I swept the floor and porch down to bare wood, and cleared out the cobwebs and dead bugs hanging from the rafters. I lugged the trailer seat cushions, pillows, and bedding out to an old clothesline and gave everything a good beating to free the dirt and rodent droppings, coughing and sneezing my head off as I did. My old T-shirts made good cleaning rags, and I borrowed one of Henry's paintbrushes to dust the delicate treasures on the wall shelves. I put the small carved animals from the cigar box on a shelf with the photograph of whoever's mama beside them, so she'd have company, though she seemed lonely still. Who was she? I wondered. What had her life been like, and whose mama had she been? Sad as she looked, she had a tender way about her, and I imagined her full of kind words and motherly attentions. Had she collected all the treasures for a child like me? Whittled the carvings herself? What had become of her and her child, and why had they left their treasures behind?

I wondered about these things as I cleaned and nailed and made the cabin my own. I'd never had a home that was mine before. Sure, I knew a drafty, one-room shack without even a toilet wasn't really a home, but the cabin made me happy. It was my home, however humble. My home, my way.

I dumped the old fireplace ashes onto the weedy garden, thinking I might try to grow vegetables or flowers in the spring. After making sure I could see a rectangle of sky at the top of the chimney, I laid a test fire in the fireplace. When the smoke went up and out like it should, I added wood from the woodpile to warm up the room. I'd found an old window screen at Henry's and used it to keep the sparks where they belonged. I filled the hurricane lamps with lamp oil I found under Henry's kitchen sink, and cleaned the colored window glass with rags and soapy well water I heated over the fire in an old pot. The glass sparkled in all its multicolored glory, and the oil lamps created fair light for reading and writing in my brand-new journal, a present from Ms. Avery.

After the snow, Ms. Avery decided to give me an independent study project, so I could work on my writing. Each week, she said, I'd find a new assignment on my desk with books she wanted me to read. She even moved my desk to the back of the room by the windows, so I could write during lessons I already knew. Now Hargrove had to contort himself if he wanted to stare.

Turned out Ms. Avery had wanted to be a writer too, but she didn't have the discipline for it. "You have to spend so much time alone," she told me, "and then you have to keep going over and over what you've written, revising. I always wanted my *first* drafts to be brilliant, but it doesn't work like that. I didn't like writing so much as *having written*."

I liked the way she said this and other things, and the way our talks seemed a meeting of like minds. Once I almost told her about the cabin in the north woods, about the treasures on the shelves and the sad woman in the picture, but I wasn't ready to talk about them yet, and Ms. Avery didn't pry. Maybe she had some of Bessie's mind-reading ability, though, because some things she just seemed to understand.

"How'd you know I'd like that book you gave me?" I asked her.

"I didn't. I gave you one I liked and hoped you'd like it too," she said.

"I did, a lot. I like orphan stories."

"Orphan stories?"

"You know, books where kids are on their own and their parents don't get in the way of their adventures."

I told her about books I loved, and not just books about orphans in the strict sense—kids with no parents, like Mary Lennox or Mowgli—but orphans of all kinds: kids with one parent, like Huck Finn or Jem and Scout Finch or Opal Buloni; kids with missing parents, like Charles Wallace and Meg; lost or stolen kids, like Peter Pan and the Lost Boys; kids like Lyra Silvertongue, whose parents might as well be dead for all the good they were; and even orphaned animals like Rascal, and grown-up orphans like Robin Hood—abandoned by King Richard, who was always off on a crusade.

"You have the instincts of a writer," she whispered in a conspiratorial voice.

She handed me a fat notebook with a red leather cover and the word *Journal* written in gold script on the front. Part of my independent study was to keep a journal. No one was to read it without my permission, including Ms. Avery, but I was on the honor system to write in it every day. My old spiral notebook was almost full, and I was grateful to have a second, nicer notebook to write in. Ms. Avery said I could keep the journal safe in the locked drawer of her desk while I was at school. She also gave me my first independent-study assignment: to put together a class presentation about what it was like to live with Henry and his sculptures.

"The kids will love it," she said, "and get to know Henry, and especially you."

That was when I was tempted to tell her about the cabin; I was so proud of it I was about to bust. Instead I wrote about it in my brand-new journal. Down deep I believed that the minute you talked about something, you risked losing it, and I couldn't chance that. The cabin was my special place, something I shared with no one.

Or so I foolishly thought.

10

The day I found out the cabin wasn't mine alone was a strange day all around.

Two weeks before Thanksgiving, winter had set in for good. Nearly every day had been freezing-rain slippery or digit-numbing cold. The light died by five in the afternoon, and between the creeping dark and the icy wet, I spent less and less time at the cabin and felt rushed and distracted when I was there. Seemed like I'd arrive, get a fire going, read or write for an hour, and then, because of bad weather or darkness, have to hurry back. I'd worked out a direct path that avoided the brambly and steep places, but it was still a fifteen- or twenty-minute hike from Henry's, and that was in good weather. I stayed at Henry's when the weather was really raw.

On that particular Saturday, I woke to a high wind rattling the windows. It gusted so bad it bowed the trees and vexed the sculptures, setting more than a few rocking and clanging. Henry was outside early staking down the ones that needed it. By midmorning, rain was pouring off the eaves in sheets, and if that wasn't misery enough, I was in bed with a cold and we were up to our eyeballs in what Fred called "bad company."

The owners of the New York art gallery that sold Henry's work had turned up unannounced right after breakfast. Mr. Sasser, the gallery's founder and an old friend of Henry's, had died the year before and left the gallery to his awful offspring, Lillian and Sid. They made me glad I was an only child.

Lillian and Sid arrived with a little white dog who had a pom-pom hairdo so silly he must have been mortified. First thing he did was head under the house and ambush the cat. There followed a yowling, caterwauling, no-contest scratch-and-tumble, after which that dog came yelping out and hid under Fred's truck, whining and nursing his brand-new face tattoo. Weather or no, I saw the cat dart off in the direction of the Padre's church. I was real put out he didn't take me along.

Fred asked Lillian six times not to smoke her little black cigarettes in the house, but she lit up anyway and tapped her ashes into her hand. "Who in blazes does she think she is?" he groused, then muttered in stronger language under his breath.

Lillian was skinny as a stick and dressed all in black. She had long, red-lacquered fingernails and wore her dyed black hair pulled so tight off her face it looked painful. She had a bossy way of talking that made me want to slap her pasty-white face. Sid, light-years away behind sunglasses, agreed with whatever she said.

She called everyone sweetheart, though I overheard her call me "that cracker child" when she was talking to Sid. When I told that to Fred, he called Lillian a word I won't write here.

He wanted to say it to Lillian's face, but I stopped him. "Sticks and stones," I told him. "As Manny used to say, 'Don't get mad, sugar boots, get *even*.'"

Having Lillian around was hardest on Henry. She followed him everywhere like a black cloud, hanging on his every word.

"Artists are *gods*," she told me, "and Henry Royster is the modern Zeus. I worship at his altar." She actually said that, I swear.

"Beg pardon?" I replied, rolling my eyes. Not that she'd notice. She never looked at people when she talked to them.

"Zeus, sweetheart," she said, like I was dumb. "Greatest of all Roman gods."

If she didn't know Romans from Greeks, I wasn't going to set her straight. Later, while she was haunting Henry in his studio, spacey Sid wandered upstairs to use the bathroom and stopped in my doorway afterward.

I glanced up from my independent study. "Done worshipping at Henry's altar?" I said.

Sid snorted. "I may know beans about art, kid, but I know which side my bread is buttered on, and so should you." He lit a special cigarette of his own, breathed the smoke in deep, then exhaled it my way, like Ray used to do. He pointed out my windows toward the sculptures in the field. "We look out there and see junk. She sees art worth a million bucks. Guess who's right?"

I didn't like Sid presuming to know what I thought. "What's this *we* stuff?" I said. "Got a rat in your pocket?"

Sid just smirked and slithered downstairs. After he went outside, I slid down the banister and locked myself in the study—the only room in the house with a bolt on the door—to read the art-magazine articles about Henry. They weren't written in anything like plain English and sounded a lot like Lillian. One talked about how Henry was "formed" as an artist ("by tragedy"), how he "developed" (in "inspired isolation," whatever that is). Another described his work as "monumental, elemental, and masterly" and Henry as "one of the great living artists of this century and the next." Well, la di flipping da.

The one with Henry scowling on the cover was as straight-forward as any. It talked about how he'd worked successfully at two careers, sculpture and cardiology, until he quit medicine to sculpt full time. But after his wife, Amanda, died of cancer, he disappeared, like he'd fallen off the earth. The art world lost track of where he was or what he was doing, and after a few years most people thought he'd died too.

When Fred came back from the store, I kept him company in the kitchen while he tenderized a rump roast. He said every time he poked it with a fork he imagined it was Lillian's behind. That made me laugh. I asked him about the articles.

"Art manure," Fred said. "That's what Henry calls it."

I smiled. "So it's not true?"

"Oh, it's truth of a sort. A high-toned, hot-air version of truth. But I wouldn't want 'em telling *my* life story."

"Henry's awful cranky today," I said.

"It's those New York bloodsuckers."

"Why does he even *talk* to them?"

"It's how he makes his living. Henry had a contract with their father, but now his contract's with Lillian and Sid. Henry owes their art gallery a fifteen-sculpture show by year's end, and they're holding him to it."

"That's less than two months away!" I said.

"And if Henry doesn't deliver, Lillian says she'll sue. She'll have her pound of Henry's flesh one way or the other."

I felt for Henry. It frosted my grapes when people tried to pull my strings like I was some kind of puppet. Mama had done that to me. When she couldn't sweet-talk her way to what she wanted, she'd say I was contrary, plain and simple, that if she said *run*, I'd walk, and if she said *walk,* I'd stand still as stone to spite her—which, come to think of it, was probably true. She liked to tell about the time when I was three and we were about to cross a busy street. She snapped, "Give me your hand," and I snapped back, "No, it's mine!"

When the art vultures flew off around three o'clock, Fred went home to Bessie, and Henry stomped out to his studio. I heard his grinder going and I let him be. He was clearing Lillian and Sid out of his system. The rain had eased up enough for me to do the same, bad cold or not. I put on my boots, coat, and a rain slicker and headed up to the cabin.

By the time I got there, though, the rain and wind had started up again. I didn't even try to light a fire. Gusts whistled down the chimney and blew ashes and rainwater all over the floor. The woodpile outside was soaked through.

I kept my coat on and sat shivering at the table, trying to record the day in my journal. But the damp pages curled, my writing hand got stiff with cold, and my head filled up with snot. I managed just half a page before I decided to read instead. I lit both oil lamps and lay in the bed fully clothed with all the old quilts pulled over me, but it was so dark outside that even with the lamps going I could barely make out the words on the page. I was cold to the bone.

It struck me then how much good light and warmth mattered to me. If I lived in that cabin all the time I'd be stuck with whatever wretchedness the weather brought. There'd be no heat when the wood got wet, and even if I managed to keep it dry, that pile wouldn't last. I'd have no warm, dry clothes when mine got wet. There'd be no home-cooked meals hot in the oven when I got home. And there'd be precious little light, especially on winter days.

I looked at my little cabin and saw it for the shack it was. The unchinked cracks in the log walls that let in the bitter cold. The floor still so filthy it might as well have been dirt. The skin of ice in the bottom of what passed for a sink. Could I really live like this? All the time? And not just one or two hours a day, but day and night, spring, summer, fall and winter, year after year? I might not miss TV, but wouldn't I miss hot and cold running water or clean clothes? Heat that I didn't have to generate myself? Electric light? Could I go without a flush toilet or a bath? Would I want to even if I could? And what would I eat? Would I steal what I couldn't grow or kill with my own hands? Could I actually *kill* an animal? Then skin, cook, and *eat* it? Would I get lonely? Would I miss having other human beings to talk to? And what if I got sick, like now? Or needed help?

I was a tangle of questions as I sniffled and shivered in that miserable bed. In my sorry state, the answers were distressingly clear. I looked up at the shelf with the sad woman's picture on it, some pitiable child's woebegone mama, and it seemed to me that even the roughest lives I'd read about in books were warmer and softer than theirs must've been.

And that's when I saw it. It was set in casually among the others, shoulder to shoulder with the squirrel and the deer. I stood up to look closer. There on the shelf, beside the picture of the woman and the six small animal carvings, was a seventh creature, a tiny wood carving of a cat, no bigger than half a walnut shell. The cat was curled up, sound asleep, in every detail like my own cat, down to his oversize head, raggedy ears, and the splotch on the right side of his tiny, perfect nose. It was beautiful. I knew at once that it was meant for me.

I picked it up and cupped it in my hands, marveling at the likeness, but then it hit me. Whoever had made it and left it there had to be watching everything I did. I whirled around, half expecting someone at the window or door, but there was only wind and rain.

I slipped the carving into my pocket and hurried back to Henry's, fingering the little wooden cat all the way. I was actually glad to see Henry's sculptures spinning in the yard to greet me and relieved to hear his welder running out back. I switched on all the downstairs lights and set the supper in the oven on warm, then sat turning the little cat in my hands, running my fingers over the curve of his back and the points of his ears. I wasn't scared, exactly. No one who meant me harm would carve me such a beautiful thing. What unsettled me was that whoever had carved the cat seemed to know me, know my daily habits and secrets, things nobody could know unless they were watching me day and night.

I heard the front door open and Henry kicking off his boots in the hall. I slipped the carving back into my pocket.

"How're you feeling?" he asked, coming in the kitchen. He scrubbed his grimy hands in the sink and put his palm to my forehead in his doctor way. He lifted an eyebrow, noticing my damp hair and clothes. "You were supposed to stay in bed."

"It was a weird day," I said.

He nodded like he thought so too, then took the roast out of the oven and set it on top of the stove. He carved off two small slices, put them on a plate with carrots and potatoes, and handed the plate to me. He made a bigger plate for himself and sat down. "I'm sorry about those people," he said.

"I'm sorrier for *you*."

"The exotic life of the artist. Now you see why I live where I do."

I rested my head on my hand and picked at my food. Pot roast and vegetables, my favorite. It all looked delicious, but I couldn't smell or taste a thing. My head felt like it was stuffed with stones. "I can't eat."

Henry set down his knife and fork. "What say I put you to bed?"

He carried me up the stairs, helped me into my PJs, and tucked me in. He brushed back the damp strands of hair stuck to my forehead, then put one hand under my head and held a glass of water so I could drink. Nobody had ever tended to me like that before. And I let him. I let him sit next to me till I drifted off.

I had a troubled, stuffed-up sleep. I woke in the night and slipped the little cat under my pillow, hoping it might sweeten my dreams. But all night long, wild scenes swirled in my stuffy head. The strangeness of the day shredded and churned my memories, then spun them like a tornado in my brain. Mama swept by on a flying hospital bed, and Ray ran past with a rifle after the white deer *and* the cat, Maud chasing after Ray. The cat was stalking a rat bigger than he was, Fred was telling Bessie and the Padre that he'd known all along that something bad would happen to me, and Lillian and Hargrove Peters were pointing at me, laughing, calling me trailer trash. Sid put one of his special cigarettes to my lips, saying, "Try this, kid, and you won't care what anybody thinks," after which Henry appeared in a white coat, shined a bright light in my eyes, and said, "She's completely crazy, like her mother; there's nothing I can do."

I woke up suddenly after that, hardly able to breathe, but when I finally fell back to sleep, I had the oddest dream of all.

This dream wasn't agitated like the others, but peaceful. And that alone was strange, because it was about my daddy. At least I thought it was him at first. I couldn't make out his face in the darkness. Like the dream before, in the woods, I just knew it was him. He stood over my bed, watching me sleep. He seemed thoughtful and curious and not in any hurry. Once, he started to reach out, but then he drew his hand back, like he was worried I might wake. He stood over me for the longest time. And the most peculiar thing was how the dream eased my mind and led me, finally, into a deep and restful sleep.

That's how, in the end, I knew it wasn't Daddy. It couldn't have been him. Because whoever it was actually *cared*.

Once the horrible people left with their mutt, he began to venture closer to the house, to be there waiting as soon as the girl got home in the afternoon.

When the weather was good, he even trailed her closer and closer to the cabin. Each day she coaxed him a little farther with bribes of roasted meat or fish from the previous night's supper. She took care not to force or frighten him, moving slowly and speaking in a low, quiet way, waiting for him to decide to move farther on.

Eventually, against his better judgment, he was shadowing her most of the way there, as far as the underside of the silver house. From there he watched, kept his eyes open, but saw no sign of the savage or his son.

Near sunset each day, he followed her back to the man's house, and after dinner, when the man returned to his shop, the cat climbed onto the man's porch. The girl sat with him there—she on the porch swing at one end, and he on a soft, dry cushion she'd put down at the other. It was just the two of them then, the cat's favorite hours.

C'mere, she would call from the house doorway or the yard or her window high up in the house. The sound of her voice was musical and sweet, and if he could hear it, wherever he was, whatever he was doing, he would come. I'm going to name you Mr. C'mere, the girl said to him one day. Mr., for respect, and C'mere, because that's what you come to. And he understood those sounds were his and his alone.

When the weather turned wintry, the girl kept closer to home. The man's helper made a small, swinging door beside the main one. The helper put a window in the little door so the cat could see in, and the cat began to lie in front of it, watching the girl's movements inside the house. The girl, on the inside, tried to urge him through it. The helper chuckled. The cat stayed stubbornly outside, though once when she was gone a long time, he pushed his head through to look around.

The days passed swiftly and began to seem much the same. The two men began early and worked late. The girl rode off with one of them most mornings and came home midafternoon. The cat stopped wondering where she was or if she would come back. She went and came back and it was simply so.

He napped in the yard or under the house, and sometimes he even hunted in the woods near the cabin. It pleased him to stalk and creep and pounce again in his old haunts, to mark the territory as his.

One day, when the girl was gone, he wandered all the way to the cabin. He scratched his back against the rough-hewn porch and warmed himself in the last rays of the sun. The air was still, and he listened with pleasure to tomorrow's breakfast rustling in the woods, the squirrels chattering in the trees, and even, far in the distance, the man and his helper hammering and grinding. But as the sun sank behind the treetops he heard another sound, familiar to him yet forgotten, from a time long ago. He sat up and pricked his ears, scanning the forest. And he was dimly aware of dark presences lurking, something that was not right.

11

When Fred and I pulled in the drive, Sheriff Bean's cruiser was parked in front of the house. He and Henry were standing in the cold down by the studio door, in serious conversation. Mr. C'mere wasn't waiting for me on the porch as usual, either. Since yesterday, he'd been cross with me, and extra wary. He flat refused to go up the path to the cabin, though he'd been following me there for a couple of weeks. He sat down stubborn as glue at the edge of the yard, refusing to move, even for Fred's corned beef.

I'd been out of sorts since yesterday myself, because some-body stole my journal from Ms. Avery's desk. I'd hardly filled twenty pages. Ms. Avery and I turned the classroom upside down without any luck. I knew who'd taken it, just didn't have proof.

The sheriff waved in our direction.

"You been speeding?" I said to Fred as we walked over.

"No, have you?" he said.

The sheriff and Henry looked serious, and when Fred and I got close enough to eavesdrop, they cut their eyes toward me and lowered their voices, the sheriff speaking urgently and fast.

Henry nodded at what he said, then glanced at me worriedly.

"Afternoon, afternoon, my good friends," the sheriff called out. "All ready for Thanksgiving tomorrow?"

"I am!" I said.

He smiled his tobacco-brown smile.

"How's Henry treating you?" he said to me, whipping out a fat pack of Juicy Fruit and offering everybody a stick. I took one and so did Fred. The sheriff unwrapped two sticks, folded them together, and stuck them in his cheek like a chaw.

"Fine for now," I told him.

"Well, keep me posted. After this weekend, Mrs. Bean and I will have four empty bedrooms again. You keep an eye on this one, too," he said, nodding at Fred.

"Oh, I do," I said, giving Fred an if-you-know-what's-good-for-you look.

Henry tossed down his greasy rag and said, "Let's all go inside where it's warm."

He cleared spaces in the studio for us to sit. Three roaring heaters made the studio toasty. He propped his foot on the first rung of a step stool and rested his elbow on his bent knee. I called it his *Thinker* pose, after a famous statue by the French sculptor Rodin. I'd seen a picture of it in one of Henry's books.

"As I was telling Henry," the sheriff said to me and Fred, "yesterday two boys stumbled on a rusty old still in the woods about a mile due north, near Henry's property line. They were hanging out there after school drinking beer and fiddling with it."

"Never knew there was a still up there," Fred said.

"What's a still?" I asked.

"For homemade liquor," he said. "A still's what you make it in."

The sheriff nodded. "The boys claim they were up there checking out an old cabin they'd heard about when they just *happened* on the beer and the still." He gave us all a skeptical look. "They say they caught sight of an albino deer hightailing it off into the woods, and then somebody shot at them with a bow and arrows. I wouldn't believe one word of this inebriated fairy tale except that one of them—Mayor Peters's boy, Hargrove—had a good-sized gash in his arm, and there was blood all over both of them."

When the sheriff mentioned the cabin and the white deer, my heart started beating fast, but when he said Hargrove's name, it pounded like it might leap out of my chest. I hadn't told Henry what had happened at school on Monday. After I'd given my Henry presentation and the class had gone to lunch, I came back to the room for a book and caught Hargrove gaping at the art books I'd left on my desk. When I asked what he thought he was doing, he froze and turned three shades of red. I went straight to *his* desk, reached inside, grabbed his dog-eared notebook, and started flipping through his pencil drawings of animals, dogs and birds and squirrels. Hargrove crossed that room like a shot, snatched it out of my hand, and shoved me against the door just as Ms. Avery walked up. She took us right to the principal's office, and Hargrove had to apologize to me in front of his daddy, the mayor. The next day my journal was gone.

Now I put on my best poker face and looked from Henry to the sheriff to Fred. Thank heaven for card nights with Manny and his gambling buddies.

"How is the Peters boy?" Henry asked.

"Doc Wilson says he won't be throwing sliders for a while, but otherwise he'll be fine."

Henry nodded. "And you say the other boy is older? A cousin?"

"That's right," the sheriff said. "I'd bet money those two were drinking and Hargrove cut himself on that old still. They got scared and concocted a story on their way home so they wouldn't get in trouble. But Mayor Peters wants me to investigate." The sheriff didn't look happy about his mission or in a hurry to accomplish it.

"Sounds like two knuckleheads on a bender," Henry said.

"I came by here to see if you'd seen anybody prowling around on your back land, especially the northern piece bordering Maud Booker's place."

Henry frowned when the sheriff spoke Maud's name, while I felt like I jumped about four feet in the air.

"Maud know about this?" Fred asked. "If even a *rumor* of a white deer gets out, hunters won't leave it alone, posted land or not."

The sheriff turned to Henry. "You ever go up there?"

"Not in forty years," Henry said. "I'd forgotten about that cabin, but it was a ruin even then. Augustus and Maud did keep a hawk's eye out for hunters and ran a few off at gunpoint."

"And she's kept it up," the sheriff said. "Nobody with any

sense hunts up that way. I warned Maud not to take the law into her own hands. What I can't figure out is how those boys knew there was a cabin to see."

"My journal!" I cried.

Henry turned to me. "What do you know about this?"

"Why, you go in that direction every day," Fred said, the fact just dawning on him.

"That's what Henry was saying before you got home," the sheriff said to me.

"I wasn't aware you went that *far*," Henry said. "What journal are you talking about?"

"My private journal that Ms. Avery gave me. Somebody stole it, and Hargrove's in my class," I said, keeping my differences with Hargrove and his daddy to myself.

Hargrove's father, the mayor, had turned out to be a grown-up version of Hargrove in a suit and tie. Hargrove shrank in his chair the second his daddy came in the principal's office. He shrank even more when his daddy caught sight of the dog-eared notebook lying wide open on the desk. His daddy frowned at the drawing—a fair pencil sketch of a Henry sculpture I'd shown in my presentation—and then slapped the cover closed and said, "I thought I told you to quit this mess and pay attention in class." Hargrove looked like a whipped dog. I even felt a little sorry for him till my journal went missing.

"Is there truth to what those boys were saying?" the sheriff asked me. "Because if you were there and had to defend yourself, they were trespassing and full of beer besides, and there won't be charges."

The sheriff looked like he was half hoping I *had* winged Hargrove. They were all three looking at me.

"I've never seen any still or boys up that way," I said honestly. "And I don't own a bow and arrow. Sounds like somebody's been reading too much Robin Hood."

"What about yesterday?" the sheriff asked. "Did you see or hear anything out of the ordinary?"

"I didn't see or hear boo yesterday. Not between having my journal stolen and my cat. He sat down at the foot of that trail and wouldn't budge."

"What cat?" asked the sheriff, looking around.

"He's under the house," Fred told him. "Only comes to her. Follows her around like a little dog. Mutual-admiration society of two."

"Well, he wasn't admiring me yesterday," I said. "Wouldn't budge for love or Fred's corned beef."

"You fed him my slaved-over corned beef!" Fred hollered.

"I'm trying to train him, Fred! Jeezy peezy!"

"I wouldn't mind laying eyes on this animal," said the sheriff, looking impressed. "Not every day you meet an honest-to-god guard cat."

"You might never lay eyes on him," Fred said. "He's a one-girl cat."

"Well, he's got good sense, I'll say that," the sheriff said to me. "And you're one hundred percent sure you didn't see anything even a little bit strange?"

"Nothing," I said.

"Well, that's good enough for me. You stay close to home

for now with your cat, and I'll have my deputy do some extra patrolling on North Road. Call me if you have one whiff of trouble, okay?"

"Will do," I said.

"Thanks, Sheriff," Henry said, though he still looked worried. "Happy Thanksgiving."

"Same to you," said the sheriff.

Fred walked the sheriff to his cruiser while Henry stayed back with me. He was working a nut up and down the threads of a bolt and studying me. "Is there anything we need to talk about?" he asked.

I hesitated. "That lady the sheriff mentioned, Maud Booker, she came here. The last time you went down to check on Bessie. She claimed to be my grandmother and said she just wanted to see if I was okay. I'm sorry I didn't tell you."

Henry nodded a little. "Do you want to talk about her now? Not that I could tell you much beyond the rumors. My father had women friends; she was one. Maud's always kept to herself, been fierce about her land and privacy."

"Later, okay?" I said. I wanted to get to my cabin, make sure everything was all right.

"At dinner, then," he said. "Anything else?"

I shook my head.

"I don't want you going up in the woods for a while," he said sternly.

"I know," I answered, nodding like I agreed as I backed out the door.

"I mean it, Zoë," he called after me. "Do you hear me?"

"I hear," I hollered back. "Loud and clear."

"If you like, I'll walk up there with you later, but I can't go now. I need to keep working on these pieces for Lillian. All right?"

"All right, Uncle Henry," I called, backing down the drive. "Do what you need to do."

Mr. C'mere came out from under the crawlspace as the sheriff's cruiser sped down the drive. We sat on the porch together until Fred drove off and Henry's grinder started up again. I thanked him for protecting me the day before and gave him the last piece of Fred's corned beef. Then I sneaked out of the yard and over the bridge, quiet and quick as I could.

She called to him, but she didn't wait for his short legs to catch up. She rushed headlong into the woods toward the cabin, her mind on other things.

Today, at least she was kind.

The day before, she'd snapped at him, trying to push him where he would not go. She'd lacked all sense of danger, while he'd caught its stink at once on the air. Couldn't she smell it? The stench reminded him of the savage, brought back the old fears.

After the boy's mother died, the savage had seemed changed. The day after his son was born, he'd buried the woman's body under the dogwood in the cabin's yard, whispering soft words. He tidied the silver house and grounds as the woman had, and tended to his son.

The cat had been a kitten then. From time to time, as he hunted in the woods, he glimpsed the boy and his father. By autumn the boy had learned to walk, and by spring he was agile and quick. The cat would come upon him in the woods, naked and laughing, chasing squirrels and birds and sometimes the cat himself, calling kitty, kitty, kitty, delighting in everything, the savage not far behind. The boy learned to pee and squat away from the house, marking his territory.

The cat marked it back. The boy learned to feed himself, stuffing his mouth with his chubby open hand and dropping half his meat on the ground for the cat.

While the boy explored, the savage rebuilt the log house not far from the silver one. Quickly a porch appeared, then two simple chairs, windows, a door. The boy watched his father work in a kind of rapture, and in the evenings, when the man pointed to the stars and to the moon rising over the tree line, he gaped at his father in amazement, as though the savage had put them there.

By the sixth winter, the savage began to leave the boy by himself more often, first locking him in the cabin alone for a few hours, then overnight. The boy cried bitterly when the man left him, and once he grabbed hold of his father's leg. The savage shook him off and ran, and the boy's short legs could not keep up.

As the boy grew older, the savage stayed gone for a day or two at a time. When he returned he was loud and rough and unsteady on his feet. He came and went on the guttering two-wheeled machine that sent the cat flying but mesmerized the boy. The boy pestered his father, who taught him to drive it and let him circle the clearing on its

back, until one day it spun out from under him and stopped.

The savage spent most days in the woods with his other contraption, tinkering. He swilled from a jar as he worked, and by afternoon's end he staggered back to the cabin and to the boy. Evenings, the savage sat in a porch chair with a knife and a piece of wood, paring off little shavings onto the ground, carving small objects. The boy watched him as if under a spell. In time, his father gave him the knife, showed him how to carve the objects himself.

One full moon, when the cat had a rabbit cornered nearby, the savage filled jars from his contraption, screwed on the lids, and packed the jars in a box. As always, the boy's eyes grew big when he saw his father leaving, though he'd learned not to beg. He stood and watched mutely as his father started out. The savage caught sight of the cat crouching in a blackberry bramble. He picked up a stone and hurled it at the cat's head. The cat bolted before it fell.

A few days later, the savage still gone, the boy started to wail. He wailed all night, and by morning the cat moved farther off to rest his ears. When the wailing stopped for a few hours at sunset, the cat crept up the trail. The boy lay sleeping in the dirt, curled into a tight ball. His face was swollen, streaked with dirt and misery.

The cat killed a rabbit and dragged it back, dropping it silently at the boy's side. He waited nearby. He thought the boy might be hungry. This time, though, the boy woke staring into the dead eyes and started up again. He clutched the stiff bunny and raged all the next day and the next.

Stupid boy, the cat thought. Didn't he know luck when he had it?

The cat kept clear of the boy after that. Sometimes he caught glimpses of him running through the woods, but until the girl came, the cat wanted no part of savage fathers or the idiot sons who worshipped them, no part of humans at all.

He watched the girl race up the path, thinking how much, today, she reminded him of the boy. By the time he arrived at the cabin, she was furious. Broken objects spilled out the door onto the porch and littered the yard. Others were stomped into the ground or crushed with large, muddy footprints.

She took in the mess, ranting, angry tears spilling down her cheeks, then squatted to pick up the bent feathers, broken eggshells, the shards of colored glass.

12

Beyond the cabin, in woods I hadn't explored, I found a rusty heap of dented metal, the remains of the old still. Pieces of it lay scattered in every direction with beer cans and cigarette butts all round.

I picked up what I could find of my treasures, but the few feathers and eggshells I found were bent or smashed to bits and the little carved animals were gone. You didn't have to be a detective to see that Hargrove and his cousin had lied up and down about what happened. They'd used the porch chairs to break the cabin windows, then tramped inside, pushed over the table and stools, stomped on the bedcovers, and left their muddy footprints everywhere. I couldn't fix the windows, but I stuffed the tattered quilts in the holes to keep out the rain and swept up most of the mud and glass. I set the broken treasures in the sink and remade the bed, trying to restore some order, though it didn't do much good. I kept pushing tears back. I wished whoever had shot at Hargrove had put that arrow straight through his heart.

Every light was on in Henry's house by the time Mr. C'mere

and I got back. A big, fancy car I'd never seen gleamed in the drive. Mr. C sniffed the tires and stayed back while I scouted ahead. Before I got to the porch I heard voices coming from the unused room at the front of the house.

Through the windows I saw that somebody had pulled the bedsheets off the furniture. It looked like a regular living room now, with all the lamps lighted and a fire burning in the fireplace. Bessie sat talking in the fireside armchair. Henry stood leaning against the mantel scowling at some faraway thing, and a man and a woman I didn't know sat on the couch, the man lying on his back with his head in the woman's lap. She was about Henry's age, I guessed, blond and pretty, with an interested expression on her face. The man held a cigarette holder with no cigarette in it, and he kept looking up at the woman.

In no mood for company, I slipped in the kitchen door to get the skinny from Fred. "I was just wondering when the ransom call would come," he said, glancing up from glazing a ham. "Henry and I have been worried sick. We were giving you ten more minutes before we called the sheriff."

"What are you talking about?" I said, taking a handful of carrot sticks from the colander.

"Henry didn't tell you?"

"I haven't talked to him yet. Tell me what?"

"Mayor Peters is offering a five-thousand-dollar reward to know who hurt his son. He says he has a good idea who it was."

"Is that a fact?" I said, wishing it *had* been me.

"It is," Fred said, lifting an eyebrow. "The mayor says you and Hargrove had words earlier this week—"

"I caught Hargrove going through my desk!"

"And you went through his."

"I can't believe what I'm hearing! Hargrove's been weird to me since the first day! He didn't like me even before I got here! He stole my journal! He—"

"All the more reason to be *careful*," Fred interrupted.

I crunched my carrot sticks, glad the steam pouring out of my ears was invisible. I'd been stupid to spend even half a second feeling sorry for Hargrove. He'd insulted me, stolen my property, and invaded my sacred place. I was beyond happy that somebody'd shot at him. That was just the start of what he should suffer for all he'd done.

"Are you listening to me?" Fred asked.

"Who're those people in there?" I said, changing the subject.

"Helen Cavanaugh and her husband, Franklin. Old, *old* friends of Henry's from New York who came to surprise him. She's a painter. And he's some hotshot writer, and a lawyer besides."

I made a face, remembering Lillian and Sid, but Fred saw what I was thinking.

"Not like that," he said. "They're good people, so you be nice. They're here for Thanksgiving. They'll stay in Henry's room, and he'll sleep out in the studio."

"He practically sleeps out there anyway," I said.

Fred gave me a dark look and slid the ham back in the oven. "Try to behave, will you? Go introduce yourself. They've been waiting on you."

I was in no mood to meet new people, but I couldn't get upstairs without going by the front room.

"Odysseus returns," said the man, standing as I came into view. I'd seen people do this in the movies, but nobody had ever stood up for me. He held out his hand, and I went over and shook it. "Franklin Cavanaugh III. Pleased to make your wily and intrepid acquaintance."

"I'm Helen," said the woman. "Just Helen. You should be flattered. Franklin doesn't stand up for any reason if he can avoid it."

"'Never stand when you can sit; never sit when you can lie down,'" Franklin said, stretching out beside her on the other two-thirds of the couch.

"I like that," Bessie said. "I'm going to write that down."

Franklin sucked on the end of his empty cigarette holder.

"There's no cigarette," I said.

"Dr. Royster forbids it," Franklin whined, giving Henry a long-suffering look.

"I say it too, but do you listen to me?" Helen said. She turned toward Henry. "Could we just move in, so Franklin will behave?"

"I can't seem to get anyone else around here to do as I ask," Henry said sharply. "Why should Franklin be the exception?" He'd looked relieved when I came in the room, but suddenly he turned to me, all annoyance. "Nice of you to join us."

"We heard about those two boys," Bessie said. "Fred and Henry were worried into next Tuesday, but I told them you were scrappy and quick and smarter than all of us put together. I'd have gone up there with you, except for the old women around here holding me back. What'd you find out?"

"Not much," I said, pleased she thought I was smart. "They made a big mess. Beer cans, cigarette butts—"

"Torture me," Franklin moaned.

"Sorry," I said.

"If you play bridge, I'll forgive you."

"I don't."

"Poker?"

"Not really."

"Gin?"

"Now you're talking."

Franklin pulled a deck of cards out of his left shirt pocket. "Dollar a point?" he said.

Helen looked at me, then at Franklin. "You two are made for each other. A *nickel* a point. I'll stake you, but later, okay?" She turned back to me. "Henry tells us you're a writer."

"I'm writing my memoir, if that's what you mean." I cut my eyes to Henry, not sure I liked everybody knowing, but not sure I didn't either.

"Franklin writes fine novels," she said. "Henry has them in his library."

"Well, I want to borrow them," Bessie said. "I like a good story."

Franklin nodded his appreciation.

"What do you write about?" I asked him.

"This and that," he said.

I turned Franklin's name over in my mind. It seemed

familiar. "Did you write a kids' book about a boy called Thaniel set after a nuclear war and he's got a ferret and a three-legged dog and he was in school in England when the bombs went off and he's trying to get home to Tennessee where his parents live?"

"I did," Franklin said, pleased.

Everyone looked at me.

"That was a good book!" I said.

"A child genius," Franklin said, "destined for great things."

"I liked the dog especially, though it was kinda sad how it ended with—"

"Don't tell how it ends! I want to read it!" Bessie said, as Fred called us to the kitchen table.

Supper was glazed ham, mashed potatoes, string beans, angel biscuits, and apple cobbler. I was relieved not to have to say much while we ate. Helen and Bessie talked a blue streak about a show of Helen's paintings at some museum, Bessie's quilting, and Fred's flower gardens. Helen talked about the similarity in the things they did. She said she'd never seen quilts like Bessie's, with such extraordinary colors and "juxtapositions." A quilt that Bessie had given her hung on the wall of her painting studio and inspired her every day. She wanted to organize a show for Bessie's quilts in New York City. Bessie tut-tutted and said that quilting came as naturally to her as breathing. The designs came straight from her heart, a gift from her angels, and Helen ought to put her quilt on the bed where it belonged. Still, I could tell she was happy that Helen thought her quilt was more than a bedspread. Fred wouldn't even entertain Helen's suggestion that his flowers were high art. He insisted he did it because he loved Bessie, for that reason and no other.

"We all have our different reasons," Helen said. "Mine are probably entirely self-serving, but I'd die if I couldn't paint."

"Die?" I said, curious. I wondered if I'd die if I couldn't read or write in my journal.

"I mean my spirit would die, everything good about me. I'm grossly unhappy and mean as a mongoose if I don't get to paint in solitude every day."

While she was talking, Franklin had hung nine spoons from his face: four from his cheeks, two more from his eyebrows, and one each from his nose, mouth, and chin. He was working on ten when Helen finally noticed. She burst into a musical laugh, like tinkling glass, and as she did, the spoons fell to the table and clattered onto the floor. We all laughed. Everyone but Henry.

He sat stiffly at one end of the table, frowning or fidgeting occasionally but not saying anything. Once or twice Helen glanced in his direction, then exchanged eye-rolls with Bessie. I tried to ignore him, glad we had company so I didn't have to hear about bows and arrows and Hargrove Peters, though I knew I'd hear plenty about them later.

After the dishes were cleared, Henry took Helen and Franklin out to his studio to show them his newest work. I excused myself and headed upstairs.

As they walked out back, I heard Helen pleading my case. "Don't punish her on Thanksgiving, Henry. For my sake?

Please." But their voices faded and I couldn't hear what Henry told her. Weird thing was, I really wanted to know what he said.

I stretched out on my bed, my room bright with moonlight. I stewed about the day and waited for Henry's lecture. Soon I heard Fred and Bessie's truck motor down the drive. Half an hour later, Franklin and Helen giggled like children as they climbed the stairs to Henry's room. I sat up, ready to argue, explain, defend myself. But Henry's welder started up out back, and he never came inside.

The next day, humans were everywhere.

The strange man and woman had stayed the night, upstairs. The helper and his mate drove up after sunrise only to drive off and come back with the gimpy old man from the steepled house down the road. The racket they made echoed in the crawlspace. They stomped and rushed around overhead, dragging and rattling things, laughing and carrying on. The cat moved to the porch. But out they came: for firewood, to roam the yard, to traipse in and out of the man's shop.

The cat fled to the yard, crossed the streambed to nap under a rhododendron. But soon one of them lumbered there, planted his wide backside on a boulder, and blew clouds of smoke that made the cat wheeze. Humans were spreading at a staggering rate, planting their fat haunches everywhere.

He went farther into the woods. But there, midafternoon, the tantalizing smell found him. It curled under his nose, wrapped around his neck like an invisible collar, knotted under his chin, and led him back to the house on a succulent leash.

It was definitely poultry, but no ordinary kind. This was wild bird, roasted and mouthwatering. The scent drew him to the yard, the house, the porch, to the plate of steaming meat. He dove in, wolfing down every juicy shred until his stomach was tight, his walk a waddle. He blessed the girl and all humankind.

A sudden hacking cough drew his attention to the drive, to a car parked some distance from the house. Smoke curled from a window. Were they all on fire? The car door creaked, then opened full, freeing a great cloud of smoke. The visitor stepped out of it, hesitant, eyeing the cat's empty dish.

Hey kitty, he said.

The girl came out then, laughing at the cat's plate licked clean.

Fred thought I gave you too much, she said to the cat. No puking now, you hear?

The car door slammed. The girl looked up, saw the visitor, and froze. He straightened and then slumped, nervy and timid both.

The girl growled, What are you doing here?

13

Harlan Jeffers. Eeyore in the flesh. Last person on earth I ever thought I'd see again.

He shivered and fisted the neck of his coat in one hand, hugging himself with the other. His eyes begged, but his pitiful act wasn't fooling me.

"I *said*, what are you doing here?"

He lowered his eyes. "I'm cold," he said.

"You're pathetic," I told him.

"That's the God's truth. I am."

"If it's money you want, you can just crawl back in your hole. Go on. Nothing for you here."

He shifted from one foot to another, looked around, his gaze settling on Mr. C'mere's plate. "That cat ate better than I did today. Or yesterday. All week, come to think."

I took him in. He *was* skinny. As skinny as I'd ever seen him. He looked about a hundred years old. My anger slackened, but only a little.

"How'd you find me?"

"Article in the paper."

"What paper?"

He pulled a crumpled newspaper clipping from his pocket and held it out to me. Mr. C scooted under the porch.

"*Farmville Times*," Harlan said. "Front page."

I took it and read: AROUND THE STATE. *Noted Sculptor Adopts Niece. Internationally recognized American sculptor and former cardiothoracic surgeon Henry Royster has petitioned the court for legal guardianship of his niece, Zoë Sophia Royster. Miss Royster is the daughter of the late Mary Elizabeth Cantrell, of Farmville, and Dr. Royster's half-brother, the late Jude Owen Royster, struck and killed by a hit-and-run driver on North Highway outside Sugar Hill. Dr. Royster and his niece reside at the Royster family home in Sugar Hill.*

"So?" I said, wondering if all Mama's deadbeat friends would show up now. I shoved the paper back at Harlan, but he wouldn't take it. I let it fall to the ground.

"Sorry I bothered you," he said. "Take care of yourself."

As he turned to go, the front door opened and Uncle Henry came out, the others right behind him. "May I help you?" Henry said. "Who is this man, Zoë?"

"Harlan Jeffers. Another one of Mama's friends wanting money."

"I'm not," Harlan said.

"What can we do for you, Mr. Jeffers?" Henry asked.

"Not a thing," said Harlan quickly, already halfway to his car. He waved over his shoulder. "Sorry I interrupted your dinner. I'll be going now."

"Henry!" Bessie called from the door in a loud whisper.

"That man's *hungry*. Don't any of you have eyes?"

"Now, Bessie," Fred warned quietly. "We don't know this man."

Bessie shot him a disapproving look. "Mr. Jeffers," she called out, "won't you warm yourself by our fire, let us set you a place at the table? We'd be thankful if you would. Isn't that right, Zoë?"

She frowned in my direction and I nodded reluctantly. "I guess. Come on, Harlan," I told him.

"I'd be grateful," he said. "I won't stay long."

I rolled my eyes. "We'll never get rid of him," I muttered as Bessie escorted him inside.

I walked out to Harlan's beat-up Ford and tried to peer in. The windows were glazed over with dirt or condensation or both, so I opened a rear door. The smell of stale cigarette smoke and ripe human being about made me faint. I drew back, fanning the foul air with my hand. The seats were piled with clothes, stuff in plastic bags, garbage, papers, and I didn't want to know what else.

"He's been living in this car," I said to Mr. C, who had followed me. "Harlan. As if there weren't enough going on. Lord."

Mr. C'mere heard them first. His ears pricked to the excited barking of dogs in the woods. He clambered quick as he could onto the pile of clothes and junk on Harlan's back seat. Voices called sharply in the trees, and I made out two or three men chasing something in our direction. I slammed the car door shut and squinted. A white blur raced through the near trees.

A second later the white deer sped wild-eyed across the yard, the drive, the field, and into the woods on the far side toward the graveyard, a gun-toting horde not far behind.

The men's shouting grew louder, the dogs' barking too. A car thundered up the drive, throwing gravel from its tires, heading straight for the house. The sheriff's cruiser screamed up behind it, the lights on its rooftop flashing. The first car veered off the drive and bumped across the field, and the squad car followed, gunning its engine, trying to pass it. Both skidded and spun out in the mud. At the same time three men carrying shotguns ran into the yard behind two barking yellow dogs with a shotgun-wielding Maud Booker bringing up the rear, everybody panting and shouting and running as fast as they could across the drive and into the field. Everybody, that is, but the dogs, who heard Mr. C yowling inside Harlan's car and swerved off to bark and scratch at the windows and doors.

Everyone inside the house poured out the front door like panicking ants from an anthill. I took the shortest route across the field, easily beating out the overweight hunters and speeding past the stopped cars. Henry and Fred and the sheriff were all shouting my name, but I wasn't stopping for anything or anybody. I got to the field's edge first and took off down the bank on my butt, scrambling toward the graveyard where the white deer thrashed bright as day inside the graveyard fence, too panicky to figure her way out.

As I got halfway down the bank, I saw somebody in there with her, trying to hold her, calm her, and work the latch on the gate all at the same time. Whoever it was must have circled around behind the house and come up behind the graveyard just as she ran inside.

"Hold on to her," I hollered as I ran. "Don't let her run!"

The person stopped fooling with the gate, threw down something that had been slung over his shoulder, and grabbed hold of the deer with both arms, exposing his broad back to the first hunter, who was just gaining the bank. I ran to the two of them as fast as my legs would go, and found myself staring into the face of wildness itself.

The stranger was tall and skinny and streaked brown as a sparrow's back with a combination of sun and dirt. His black hair hung down his back in matted hanks, tied off at the nape of his neck with a piece of leather. He wore boots scuffed up with rough work, a moth-eaten brown sweater, and a pair of loose-fitting green coveralls dirtier than Henry on his filthiest day. A worn canvas bag lay on the ground where he'd thrown it so he could get a better hold on the deer. Something peeked out of the top. It looked like the upper part of a strung bow, though I couldn't be sure.

As I stared into his face I saw a double dose of anxiety and fear, and other feelings so jumbled they made my head hurt. And that's when I knew he was the one I'd sensed in the woods whenever I saw the white deer. Not an animal at all, but a boy. A teenaged boy.

He was staring over my shoulder. I whirled back around to see the first hunter pointing his gun at all three of us, calling to his friends to hurry up and come. I glanced back at the boy and saw his expression change from scared to furious. He struggled mightily to keep the little deer's body covered with his own. She had cut herself on one of the fence spikes as she tried to jump out, and a patch of bright blood was spreading on the inside of a pink haunch. She was frantic with fear, pulling the boy this way and that, desperate to get away, though he gripped her firm. The hunter steadied his aim, not caring if anything stood in his way. He was smiling, salivating over his prize.

"Get out of the way!" he called to us as his hunter friends joined him.

"No!" the boy shouted, his voice angry and deep, like a lion's roar.

The boy and the deer were behind one of the gravestones, which shielded them from the knees down. I planted myself between that hunter and the boy's exposed back, then raised my arms and waved them frantically over my head to make the biggest possible target.

"Zoë! What in God's name do you think you're doing?" Henry thundered from above.

Henry was half running and half falling down the slope toward us. The others were lining up on the rise behind him: a panting Maud Booker, her shotgun trained on the hunter pointing his gun at us; the sheriff and his deputy; then Fred, Franklin, and Helen, with Bessie and the Padre slowly bringing up the rear, both of them leaning heavily on Harlan, who shouted, "That's my Zoë! You give 'em what-for, darlin'!"

I'd never been so scared in my life. Ray had shown me that hunters thought they owned the outdoors and everything in it, but I hadn't truly believed it till I was staring down the double barrel of a shotgun. That hunter stood his ground, looking straight at us through his sights, but as the witnesses multiplied, his sureness faltered. He glanced nervously at Maud and her gun, then at his hunter buddies, who'd stepped back and off to one side, then at the sheriff, who unsnapped the top of his gun holster, fingered the pistol butt, and yelled loud and clear, "Everybody stop right where they are!"

And everyone did. Everyone but Henry.

He kept barreling down the hill like a charging bear. The deer's panic escalated behind me, the boy having to work harder as Henry came.

"Stop, Uncle Henry, please!" I shrieked.

To Henry's everlasting credit, he did. But he looked mad enough to breathe fire.

"Zoë," he said loudly, as grim-faced as I'd ever seen him. "I want you to come here. *Now.*"

"I can't, Uncle Henry."

"This is not a discussion," Henry said firmly.

"I'm sorry, Uncle Henry," I hollered. "You can send me back to that hospital or wherever they send bad kids, I don't care. But I'm not moving."

Fred shook his head and muttered some exasperation I couldn't hear, but Henry just stood there staring at me, like I'd pushed him way past exasperation or even fury. Finally a resigned look passed over his face, and he did something that will impress me for the rest of my days. He walked sidelong down the hill, very slowly, till he was maybe ten feet in front of me, and put himself directly between me and that hunter's gun.

He turned to face me then, his back to the hunter. He looked steadily at me. Not angry, not upset. Dead serious, though. Then he turned around so we faced that hunter—together.

For the longest minute of my life, the hunter stood sighting us down the barrel of his gun, Henry still as death and staring back at him. I glanced behind me. The deer was pop-eyed with fear and wanting to bolt from hunters and barking dogs—all of us. The boy, too. Everybody kept still, watching me and Henry and the hunter. Time slowed, and even the birds seemed to hold their breath.

The hunter's shoulders finally slumped. He lowered his gun and dropped his eyes. Sheriff Bean walked over and took the gun without any fuss.

Then the sheriff turned to everybody. "My Thanksgiving dinner is at this moment growing ice-cold on Mrs. Bean's much-fussed-over dining room table." Then he turned to the hunter. "Curtis, you and your friends are going to give all your firearms to my deputy. Provided each one of you can produce a valid hunting license, you may pick up your firearms at the sheriff's department first thing in the morning. Everyone not invited to dinner at Dr. Royster's will now go home to enjoy Thanksgiving Day with your friends and relations."

"That woman chased us with a gun!" one of the hunters shouted. "We weren't even on her land. We were up by Lenter's Creek—"

"Putting you on my posted land," Fred cut in.

"Not Lenter's Creek," barked another hunter. "Big Woods."

"Church property," called the Padre.

"The mayor'll hear about this," Curtis said, pointing at me. "That girl shot at the mayor's son. I'm claiming the reward right here and now."

The sheriff sighed. "When you call His Honor, you tell him that I'm beginning a thorough investigation into *everything* that's happened here, and that I will no longer be taking the tender ages and clean records of those involved into consideration. So everybody here better get their stories straight and tell the mayor, his boy, and his boy's cousin to do the same. I'm taking statements at the first of the week, and this time, *anybody* determined to be lying or withholding facts will be looking at a charge of obstruction. And that goes for any eleven-year-old spitfires who've been keeping entirely too much information to themselves," he said, aiming that last part directly at me.

Then he pointed at the boy. "And you, young man. You make sure I get your name and address."

For a second nobody moved.

"Well, go on now, get!" he barked, "before I haul in the lot of you for trespassing, reckless endangerment, ruining my turkey dinner, and whatever else applies."

Everyone did as the sheriff asked, Maud reluctantly adding her shotgun to the deputy's growing arsenal. Henry climbed the hill to have a word with Maud. I turned back to the boy and the deer. My eyes moved to the bow peeking out of that canvas bag on the ground inside the fence, a bow nobody else seemed to have seen. The sun was sinking down behind the trees, taking the light with it. When Henry started back down the hill, I ran to meet him, wanting to give the boy a chance to calm the deer and get away if he could.

"Who is that boy, Zoë?" Henry asked right off. He spun me around and gave me a thorough look-see to make sure I was all right. I turned as slowly as I could.

"I'm as curious as anybody," I said. "First I ever saw of him was today."

Henry stayed quiet, studying me, as if he was trying to decide whether he believed me or not. "After dinner," he said finally, "the two of us are going to talk."

I heard the sound of a lone owl's hooting behind me then, and turned to see the gate open, the graveyard empty, the boy and the deer gone.

14

Manny used to drink at a hole-in-the-wall bar called Andy's, owned by a man of the same name. It had four or five vinyl-covered booths, and every night at six o'clock Andy would dim the lights, clip on a black bow tie, and turn Andy's into André's, where everything cost a dollar more. I thought about Andy's during what was left of Thanksgiving Day, because after what had happened outside, everything and everybody looked different to me.

Maybe it was the candles Helen lighted on the "table" Henry had put together earlier from three sawhorses and a piece of plywood covered by two bedsheets. Or maybe it was the mismatched plates and utensils Bessie set out—"orphans," she called them, like me. She and Helen speculated about their previous owners while they shifted and fiddled and fussed with the arrangement like they were making high art. Maud Booker ran home for an extra place setting of silverware while Franklin made place cards by writing our names on little paper parasols he found in a kitchen drawer. He even made one for Mr. C'mere and stuck it in his cat-food bowl on the porch. The finished table was beautiful like a crazy quilt and looked as sundry as our group: fine china right next to chipped everyday, crystal wineglasses next to jelly jars with ducks on them; forks, knives, and spoons with every manner of handle; and Bessie's mama's lace-trimmed cloth napkins beside Henry's multicolored bandannas from the hardware store.

Everybody was talking about what had happened, and about the boy, asking if anyone else knew him or if they'd seen the white deer before. Bessie said that, much as she hated to say it, those migrant children all looked alike to her and we had no shortage of them in Sugar Hill. Maud said the deer looked considerably less than a year old, which was likely why nobody had sighted her till now. And the Padre said that if either one of them lived nearby, neither one was a churchgoer.

Bessie shooed Harlan upstairs, insisting he make bosom friends with a washcloth and a bar of soap before joining our table. Harlan seemed more beaten down than ever before, full of shame, and his expression begged forgiveness for things I didn't even know. I heard both the shower and the tub running, and Helen dropped his old clothes down the stairwell. They about stood up on their own. She plucked up each stinky item between two fingers and carried it at arm's length past the washer and out to the trash, then sent Henry upstairs to find something for Harlan to wear.

Harlan came down scrubbed raw and wearing some of Henry's cleaner clothes, which is to say they'd been through the wash and didn't have too many grease stains or burn holes in them. With his wet hair slicked back, he looked like

Andy after he'd put on his bow tie and become André—both the old Harlan and the new improved version at the same time. Being clean seemed to lift his spirits. I couldn't say it was *good* to see him, because of the memories he brought back of Mama, but he'd scrubbed off most of his shamefaced look with the stink and dirt, and I found I didn't mind his being here so much.

I spied Maud outside sweet-talking Mr. C'mere, who was regarding her from the far side of the porch—a good thing, because he reeked of Harlan's stinky car. I went out to thank her for standing up for the white deer. She was hunkered down, telling Mr. C what a handsome devil he was, and his tail was swishing back and forth like he was eating up every word.

"Thanks for what you did," I said, squatting next to her.

She shook her head sadly. "Those yahoos'll shoot anything that moves."

"You think he'll ever let me touch him?" I asked.

She tipped her head. "Hard to tell with the wild ones, but I got a good feeling about this one. He's already come this far, seems to know he's getting old. In my experience, one day he'll just decide."

"Decide?" I asked.

"Between being alone or being befriended. The wild ones never completely tame, but I'd say he's moving in the befriended direction."

"His ear got better," I said, pointing. His eyes had closed now, but his tail still swept the floor at the sound of our voices.

"I thought it might."

"You have animals?"

"Four cats, a possum, and a crippled dog."

"How'd he get crippled?" I asked.

"Found him by the roadside, hit by a car."

"Oh," I said, thinking of my daddy. Maybe she was thinking about him too. Maybe someday I could ask her what else she knew about him, but I didn't know how to start that conversation now or if she'd mind.

"Maybe you'd like to meet them sometime," she said as we stood and headed inside.

"Maybe I would," I said.

We all sat down to our crazy-quilt table laden with roast turkey, pecan stuffing, buttered green peas, candied yams, and steaming cornbread with real butter, the sight of which made Franklin kiss Fred's hands.

Bessie offered grace, saying how thankful we were for God's beautiful wild creatures, for the sheriff and peaceful resolutions, and for the great pleasure of sharing our bounty with Ms. Booker and Mr. Jeffers. Then she looked at me and Henry, adding that it was her fond hope that our gratitude might bring out our better selves and keep all Hades from breaking loose until after dessert.

Everybody seemed to relax after that. The conversation was light during dinner, mostly about how good the food was. Harlan sat between me and Bessie, shoveling food into his mouth as fast as he could swallow it, till I kicked him under the table and he smiled, red-faced, and slowed down. He put away two good-sized platefuls, five pieces of cornbread, and two slices of pumpkin pie with whipped cream, taking the last piece under the nose of a dismayed Franklin, who'd eaten nearly as much.

"You two are a pleasure to cook for," Fred told them, seeing Franklin's face. "There's another pie in the kitchen, so nobody has to be shy. I'll go get it."

Henry followed Fred into the kitchen and came back with a bottle of apple spirits, which he poured into small glasses for those old enough, except Harlan, who said he'd sworn off the demon in a glass.

Bessie lifted her glass and the others did the same. Harlan and I raised our chocolate milk. The candlelight made everything sparkle.

"To brave children," she said, looking at me, and I felt blood rush to my face. "Those present and not."

"Rash children," Henry said, frowning.

"*Fool* children is more like it," Fred said. "Could've been killed or got us killed. Curtis is a terrible shot. Shot off half his big toe last year hunting quail."

Bessie reared back suddenly in her chair, her face hardening with real anger. "Why, Henry Royster and Fred Montgomery!" she snapped, slapping the table with her palm. "I can't believe what I am hearing."

I'd never heard Bessie raise her voice to Henry or Fred before, and by the table's reaction I guessed nobody else had either.

Fred was truly startled. "What?"

"You especially. Calling the children fools," she said. "Of all people."

"What do you mean?" he said.

"Why, you old hypocrite!" Bessie stared open-mouthed at her husband as though he was an utter stranger speaking in tongues.

"What are you talking about?" I asked her.

"I'm talking about the other fool children at this table."

"Who?" I said, looking around the table and seeing none.

"Fred Montgomery, for one. Who's forgotten he was a fool child once himself. And you, too," she said to Henry.

"Leave me out of this," Henry told her.

"Don't be digging up old dirt," Fred said.

Bessie ignored them both and turned to me. "The reason Fred, Henry, and the sheriff are friends," she began, "is that Fred and Henry saved Garland Bean's life."

"Who's Garland Bean?" I asked.

"The sheriff, honey," she said. "Garland's his given name."

"It was Henry more than me," Fred said, dismissing the whole business with a wave of his hand.

"The heck it was," Henry protested. "You brought him up. I couldn't have done my part under water."

"You dove in same as I did," Fred said. "And I wouldn't have seen him down there except for you pointing him out."

"It was both of you saved that little boy," Bessie insisted.

"What little boy?" I asked impatiently. This confused talk was making me irritable.

"Garland *Bean*, honey," said Bessie. "He wasn't but five years old when they saved him."

"That'll do, Bessie," Fred said.

"Really," Henry put in.

"Oh, tell us, Bessie," Helen said, looking at Henry and Fred. "So many heroes in our midst. I never knew."

"I'm not bothering to make up plots for my books anymore," Franklin announced. "I'll just come to Henry's and write down what I see and hear."

"I got first dibs," I told him, with a cautionary glare.

"I remember that rescue," Maud said, nodding. "Must've been forty years ago. But I thought the Wilson and Peters boys saved him. Didn't they get medals?"

"That was the story in the Sugar Hill paper," Bessie said sourly. "But that was only because the mayor's daddy owned it. The truth was buried in the state paper a week later, where nobody saw it."

"If I recall," said the Padre, concentrating, "it happened right after I first came here. A group of children were playing above the basin in the old quarry, their swimming hole. They were diving into it."

"Garland didn't dive in," Fred said. "He was shoved off that rock by two drunk high school boys."

"Delray Peters was one," Bessie said.

"Who's that?" I said.

"The mayor," the Padre whispered.

It was hard for me to imagine the mayor as a boy, but the behavior fit the family.

"Garland couldn't swim," Fred went on. "Had no business being up there in the first place. Bessie and I were on the far side of the basin, having a little time to ourselves. I heard him scream as he fell. Hit the water like a stone. I did what anybody would."

"Anybody!" Bessie scoffed. "Not a one of those other anybodies dove in after him. Not even his own brother and sister. They just stood up there shouting the fact of it, crying and calling his name, like he'd rise up out of that water on his own. But I never saw anybody move as fast as my Fred. He ran like he was afire and dove right in. Took those bystanding children clean by surprise. They hadn't even known we were there."

Bessie closed her eyes and trembled. "They were under water so long, I shiver to remember. The surface got smooth as glass. And then Fred shot up to the surface like a geyser, the first time without the boy. He took a terrifying breath, loud and desperate, then dove right back under for an even longer time. I was sure they were both dead. Then Henry shoots by out of nowhere and dives in after Fred. What were you doing up there anyway?" she said, turning suddenly to Henry.

"My motives weren't pure," Henry said. "I went up there to draw, because that's where the high school girls would go skinny-dipping. Best life-drawing class I ever had."

Harlan chuckled.

"What happened then?" I asked, not caring a bit about skinny-dipping girls.

"Next thing I knew," Bessie said, "Fred and Henry shot up out of that water, with Garland. Fred was gasping and coughing up water, but Garland looked pale as death, not breathing at all. I ran down to the water's edge and the two of them pushed

Garland high enough so I could drag him by his shirt collar to level ground, but he still wasn't breathing. Henry told Fred to work his legs, push his knees into his chest, while Henry leaned over him, lifted his little chin, and breathed the breath right back into him, alternating with that heart-pumping thing they do."

Bessie crossed her small hands over her heart and pushed up and down.

"A miracle," the Padre said to Henry.

"A merit badge," Henry said blandly.

"To top it all off," Bessie went on, "those high school kids came down and start taking credit, like it was them that pulled Garland out, especially that Lucinda Bean, Tate's and Garland's sister, who was supposed to have been babysitting Garland at home. She'd brought him up to the quarry because she was sweet on the Wilson boy."

"The lady from the grocery store?" I asked Henry, and he nodded. "She's the sheriff's sister?"

"She is," Bessie said. "Not one bit changed, if you ask me. Standing there saying Delray Peters had pulled Garland out and Willie Wilson had breathed the life back into him—as bald a bald-faced lie as ever was told, because the pair of them stood there dry as dust with Fred and Henry dripping wet beside them. They didn't even have the sense to get wet before the law came! Anybody with eyes could have seen who the real heroes were. Garland was clinging to Fred like Fred was his mama. Fred had to ride in the ambulance because Garland wouldn't let go. *He* knew who'd pulled him out. But Lucinda and Delray hold to their version to this day."

"So that's why she and the mayor don't like you two," the Padre said to Henry and Fred.

"But they saved a little kid's life!" I cried.

"No good deed goes unpunished," said Franklin.

"Unpunished by who?" I asked.

"God. The Fates. Other people. Take your pick."

"Lord," I said. "I'll never understand God or human beings as long as I live."

"Join the congregation," said the Padre.

"So much bravery here," Helen said. "I'm a sissy myself."

"Not true. You married *me*," Franklin said sweetly, and Helen smiled.

"Well, I certainly don't deserve to sit in such courageous company," said the Padre.

"Now, Padre," Bessie protested. "Dalton Pendergrass told me how you stood up to those old biddies who wanted to poison Zoë's cat!"

"Who wanted to poison my cat?" I shouted. "I'll skin 'em, I swear."

"I'll hold them down while you do," said Maud.

"Don't you worry," Bessie said. "The Padre told them they'd spend eternity in Hell if they laid so much as a fingernail on that animal. Didn't you, Padre?"

"Did I?" said the Padre hopefully. He sat up taller in his chair. "I'm so pleased."

"I want names," I demanded.

"Shhh," Henry said. He put one finger to his lips and glanced over at Harlan, and I turned to see why he'd been so quiet during the story. He was slumped back in his chair, sound asleep, head cocked to one side, his mouth full open. It was not a pretty sight.

"That man needs a dentist," Bessie said, frowning.

Henry looked at me. "What do you say we have our talk?"

The others talked on in the front room as Henry and I put out a sleeping bag and pillows in front of the study fireplace for Harlan. I settled in one of the two armchairs while Henry lighted a fire.

"Fred thinks I've let you run wild," Henry began, taking a seat behind his desk.

"Is that what *you* think?" I asked.

He considered for a minute. "See this?" he said, pointing to his forehead.

I leaned close. I saw the faintest line of a scar on his forehead, like a windy river on a map. It disappeared under his red bandanna, which he pulled off, revealing his baldness. The scar ran almost to the back of his head.

"Seventy-seven stitches," he said. "I wasn't paying attention one day. A sculpture fell on me. I hadn't distributed the weight of the upper parts properly over the base. Sliced a nasty gash in my head."

"I'm sorry," I said, not seeing where this was going.

"Fred says I haven't been paying enough attention to you. Says I've given you too much freedom, that I've been too involved in my work. He thinks things might all come crashing down on our heads. After today, I think he might be right."

"I've been on my own my whole life," I said defensively. "I've done pretty well."

"You have," he agreed. "But you've done it keeping everybody in your life at arm's length, trusting no one. Today you took a terrible risk."

"You should talk!" I protested. "Besides, I trust you!"

"Zoë," Henry said flatly, "that cat of yours trusts me more than you do."

It stung when he said that. I looked down at my lap, not wanting to look him in the eye.

"Is there anything else you want to tell me?" he asked.

I thought about the bow peeking out of the boy's bag. The last thing I wanted to do was get him in trouble.

"You said you didn't know that boy," Henry said.

"I don't," I told him. "But I've seen that deer in the woods between here and the cabin, three times counting today, and each time I had the feeling that another animal was with her, one I couldn't see."

Henry nodded.

"Until today, I thought it was just another deer."

"Anything else?"

"You know that old cabin?"

He nodded again.

"I'd fixed it up, made it nice. But Hargrove and his cousin went up there and tore everything up, broke the windows, stole my stuff, wrecked everything I'd done. I wrote about the cabin in my journal. The one that got stolen."

The phone rang then, and Henry answered. Sheriff Bean. While they talked, I tried to picture the sheriff being five and Fred and Henry being the boy's age. I thought of the boy and the white deer alone in the woods tonight. After today, I didn't hold out hope for that deer to survive hunting season. I hoped they were all right for now.

Henry hung up the phone. "The sheriff says from what little anybody in town knows, that boy's a transient, in and out of the migrant community, a picker, probably illegal." He stood up, came around his desk, and stood over me, looking serious. "I need to get back to our guests. Will you promise to think about what we've discussed, *please*?"

"I promise, Uncle Henry," I said.

"Then I'm going to trust that you and I can work this through in our own way," he told me. "All right?"

"Okay."

"Coming with me?"

"Not just yet," I said, and he nodded once and went out.

I headed upstairs without saying good night. Bessie was still fussing, telling Fred he'd forgotten what it was like to be young. I took the little carved cat from my nightstand and turned it in my hand. I'd completely forgotten to tell Henry about it. But what could I have said? I wondered now if the wild boy had made it and the others Hargrove had stolen, or if he knew who had. I thought about the crazy events of the day, about Harlan showing up and Maud with her possum, cats, and crippled dog, about Henry and Fred saving little Garland, but most of all about the boy and his deer. Seemed like I had the pieces of a puzzle, if only I could see how they fit together.

I took the small book called *The Boy Who Drew Cats* from my bedside table drawer. I opened it and looked at the pictures, trying to quiet my mind, but the story had the opposite effect. I liked it so much I read it twice, about the Japanese boy who drew cats everywhere, on walls, in books, on furniture, because he couldn't help it, because he had "the genius of an artist," and how his cat drawings came to life one night to kill the goblin rat and save his life.

Before I turned out my light, I slipped the book and the cat carving under my pillow, so I could reach for them in the night.

15

After Thanksgiving, Bessie pressed Henry into hiring Harlan to put the cabin right. Everybody but me liked the idea right off. Harlan would bunk with the Padre and help out evenings at the church, while working days at the cabin and providing what Henry called "a presence" in the north woods. That was the deal Henry struck with the sheriff and the condition he set for me. I could go up to the cabin and wander the woods so long as Harlan was around.

The mayor let his reward offer stand: Any squealing no-account could collect five thousand dollars for proof of who'd hurt Hargrove. The sheriff thought Maud had winged him, and I'd kept the boy's bow a secret. There'd been no sign of him or his deer since Thanksgiving. They seemed to be long gone.

My journal never turned up either. At the request of the mayor, Mr. Reardon moved Hargrove to another fifth-grade class, which suited me fine. Except for glimpses of Hargrove at recess, lunch, or assemblies, I hardly saw him anymore. Mad as I was about the cabin, I had better things to do than spend any more energy on someone that hateful and weird. If he stared at me across the playground or came anywhere near me in the halls, I just sidled up to Shelby or one of my other classmates and started up a conversation. I went about my business as though I was deaf, dumb, and blind to his existence—until one strange day right before Christmas break.

Thursdays Uncle Henry spent the day volunteer-doctoring at the Sugar Hill free clinic, picking me up at school afterward. He was always late, though, and on this particular Thursday he was later than usual. I didn't mind. I went around behind the school to see Sparky, who belonged to our custodian, Mr. Sylvester. Sparky was a little brown mutt-terrier, sweet and loyal. Mr. Sylvester had rescued him from a traffic island on a California freeway. Sparky was pacing the island back and forth, trapped by traffic going seventy and eighty miles an hour on either side. Seeing Sparky's trouble, Mr. Sylvester got off at the next exit and circled back around, and when he pulled off on the left shoulder and opened the door, Sparky hopped right in. He'd been riding shotgun for Mr. Sylvester ever since.

I could hear Sparky whining and barking as I went around behind the school. Mr. Sylvester always tied him to a mulberry tree in the back, where he waited patiently for his savior to quit work. As I turned the corner, I saw he'd gotten his leash wrapped tight around the tree, entangling his back legs. Somebody whose face I couldn't see was hunched over Sparky, talking baby talk to him and helping him get free. Untangled at last, Sparky rolled on his back and wriggled with pleasure as he got a stomach scratch from none other than Hargrove Peters. Hargrove seemed to be enjoying the experience as much as Sparky.

"Good boy," Hargrove was saying in a soft voice I'd never heard him use before. "Wish my daddy'd let me have a cute little dog like you," he crooned. "We could have all kinds of adventures together, couldn't we, boy? We'd go camping and fishing. I could draw your picture and you could sleep in my bed. But Daddy says mutts are common and people would laugh at a boy who had a mongrel or rescued a dog from the pound."

A sad look came over Hargrove's face when he told Sparky that. But he bucked right up again when he switched to scratching Sparky behind his ears, sweet-talking him all the while. I stood dumbfounded, hardly believing my ears or eyes, trying to make sense of what I saw. Mr. Sylvester peered out the rear doors then, to see what all the noise had been about, just as Henry's pickup pulled up behind me in the school parking lot.

I didn't know what to think about having Harlan around again, either. At first I felt like I'd gone back in time to a place I didn't care to revisit. But I had to give him credit. Within two weeks he'd cleaned the trailer till it shone, fixed the cabin's windows, rechinked the logs, and replaced the rotted porch boards, and in his spare time he was overhauling the old motorbike he'd found on the cabin's front porch. He said he'd teach me to drive it once he got it working, but I'd put him off so far, saying I'd see.

He was tinkering with it one Saturday morning when I walked up the path.

"Hey, Harlan," I said.

He looked up from where he sat on the ground, six or eight

greasy metal parts in front of him. He set down his wrench and wiped his hands on a rag. The rest of the motorcycle was leaning against the trailer. Mr. C'mere, poking along behind me, crawled underneath the trailer to sleep.

I handed Harlan a grocery bag full of sandwiches and fruit Fred had sent, and he set them inside the door. "You sure are thin," I said.

"I know it." He looked down at his belly that still curved in rather than out. "Drinking did that, and it won't put back on. Them church ladies been feeding me like a pig."

I stood there, not knowing what else to say.

"If you want me to go, I will," he said, like it had been on his mind.

I didn't say anything. If he'd said that on Thanksgiving, I'd have said fine, go, good riddance. But Bessie said Harlan was a stray like Mr. C, and as deserving of our kindness.

"I was wanting—" he began and stopped. He looked down at the ground like he was searching for something he'd lost.

"What?"

"I don't know how to put it." He studied his feet and sighed. "I ain't got words like you do."

"Say feelings, then."

He thought. "I want to say I'm sorry, but I don't know what to be sorry for. Oh heck, that's not right."

I waited.

He sighed and started again. "I'm sorry about your mama dying the way she did and I'm sorry I couldn't do more for you while I was with her."

"You did what you could," I offered, not really meaning it.

"But it didn't do no good!" he said, shaking his head. "That's what I mean to say. I just want you to know how sorry I am. If I can do something now, I'll do it, even if that something is leaving."

He looked me straight in the eye, waiting. I couldn't bring myself to be hard. "It was like it was," I said, looking away.

"I know it," he said. "But it ain't right. For a smart kid like you, I mean. You got a good way of looking at things. I admire that."

It pleased me a little when he said that, I don't know why.

"So you just say the word and I'm gone. You're doing real good and I don't want to mess with that."

Negative as I felt toward anything having to do with Mama, I couldn't tell somebody that pitiful to get lost. "Harlan?"

"What?"

"Was there good in Mama?" I asked.

"You mean something good about her or something she was good at?"

"Either."

He stood up, walked over to the trailer for his water bottle, and sat down on the middle step. He went quiet, sipping and thinking.

"That's what I thought," I said, turning to go to the cabin.

"Now, wait a minute, hold on," he said, a little curtly. "I've killed a lot of brain cells since that time. She could be real funny, I remember; she liked to laugh. And she had a pretty voice. One night you had an earache and I remember she sang to you. She sang a long time, too. Rocked you and sang till you fell asleep."

"I don't remember."

"You might not. You were bad off."

"What did she sing?"

"Let me see now." He hummed a little, but he wasn't musical. "I can't pull it up. Something pretty, though. She didn't sing much, said it reminded her of her own mama, made her sad."

"I don't remember very much," I said. "Right after she, you know, died, Ray took all her stuff to the dump. Everything. He was real mad. I didn't really blame him."

"Even so, it was mean to throw everything away."

"I don't know. I might've done it myself if he hadn't. Taking all those pills was a rotten thing to do."

Harlan looked far off. "It sure was that," he said. "But I guess you could look at it that if she hadn't done what she did, you wouldn't be here."

"What?"

"God, I shouldn't've said that," he said, suddenly disgusted with himself. "Should've kept my mouth shut. Never have been stop signs between my brain and my mouth."

"No, I want to hear. What do you mean?"

He stared off in the distance and slowly shook his head. "Let it lie. Let it all lie."

"Please," I said.

He turned back to me. "All right. You want to know, I'll tell you. I spent nearly a year with your mama, and the first half of that year was passable, she and I had some fun. She was real pretty and good company as long as she was getting her way. But the last half of that year was the worst time of my life. Where *she* was concerned, I mean. By then I wasn't staying for her, I was staying for you."

"Me?"

He nodded. "I kept thinking that however bad her drinking and drugging and lying and meanness and craziness were for me, it was your whole life to you, all the life you knew. I even went to a lawyer one time to see if I could get you away from her, but he just laughed in my face and said, 'Not a chance.' His exact words. So, all I'm saying is, bad as what she did was, her doing it cut you loose. Brought you to Henry."

Just then I had a picture of how I'd be living now if Mama was alive. She'd still be sick and not doing anything about it, in and out of the hospital, bringing home one bloodsucking boyfriend after another, one step ahead of the bill collectors and the law—thinking only of herself. I thought of Henry standing between me and that hunter's gun, putting my life before his own, something Mama had never done.

"Henry's good people," Harlan said. "Not like some."

I didn't know what to say.

"Maybe the Padre's right," he went on, an edge in his voice. "He says, 'Where there's life, there's hope.' Maybe that's right, but I can't believe it about your mama, knowing her like I did. Even if you weren't here with all these good people, even if you were in some home, or out there on your own, you'd be a million times better off without her in your life. Maybe that's a hard thing to hear, but I believe it. Maybe the best thing about her is the second chance she give you. Maybe that's the good in her you're looking for. And maybe she didn't give it to you on purpose, but so what?"

I stood there staring at him. "You really went to a lawyer?" I asked.

"Cost me a week's pay."

"You really stayed just for me?"

"Till she kicked me out."

"I never knew."

He shrugged. "Now you do."

"Thanks, Harlan," I said. "You don't have to be in any rush to go, okay? The cabin's looking real nice."

He smiled crookedly. "I appreciate that."

Harlan headed down the path to borrow some tools from Henry. I shimmied underneath the trailer, where Mr. C was curled up, asleep.

"And you think you know people," I said.

Two minutes later they came. I heard them before I saw them, both of them all care and apprehension, especially him. I saw his work boots and the raggedy cuffs of his coveralls and her slim legs and ash-gray hooves right behind. He dipped a drink of water from the well and set it down for her. I admired that. As she lowered her head into the bucket, her pink eyes caught sight of me under the trailer. She didn't seem to mind me. I could only see him from the knees down, but he was facing the cabin, and I guessed he was taking in the improvements. He went inside, and after a few minutes he came out and stood in the yard facing me, like he'd known I was there all along. I inched forward, out from under the trailer, waking Mr. C as I did. He took one bug-eyed look at the boy and the deer and bolted into the woods toward Henry's. I kept still so they'd see I wasn't a threat.

The boy seemed perfectly calm. He looked much like he had on Thanksgiving: dirty all over but not minding. It had the effect of blending him into the land and trees. His long black hair was flecked with leaves and pulled back off his face. He looked fourteen, maybe fifteen. His dark eyes studied me, and I saw then the purplish rings underneath them, how worn-out he looked, like somebody who hadn't slept in a while.

We stared at each other. I tried to think what to say, how to start a conversation with a complete stranger I already knew.

"I'm Zoë," I said lamely.

He nodded. He'd probably heard Henry and everybody else shouting it on Thanksgiving Day.

"I live just south of here with my uncle Henry, the bearded fella who makes all the big metal contraptions in our yard."

"Wild things," the boy said, nodding again.

"Wild things," I repeated, smiling. "I've been coming up here regular for a while now."

"Saw you the day you came," he said, something like amusement in his face and tone. "Most days since."

"Is that a fact?" I said. "Well, I didn't see you, not till Thanksgiving, but I've felt you nearby a few times when I saw your deer, except I—"

"You didn't!" he scoffed, interrupting. He took the strap of his canvas bag off his shoulder and let it drop to the ground.

He slid something from his pocket and sat down cross-legged in the dirt. He opened a pocketknife and started whittling on a little piece of wood. "You didn't even wake the night you got lost and I carried you home. Isn't that right, Sister?" he said, glancing at the deer over his shoulder.

"You?" I said. "But I thought—"

"Or the other time when you were sick and I watched you. Walked right in and up the stairs, nobody the wiser."

"But I dreamed that!" I said, feeling my heart beat faster.

"Or the day those two boys came up here looking for you!"

"Me?"

He nodded. "I fixed them!" Full of pride, he burst out laughing.

I blushed a little, feeling uncomfortable and foolish. "Well, then, I guess you know everything," I said a bit sharply. "Nothing I can tell you. Not one thing."

I sat quietly and folded my hands in my lap. A bit of fear and worry crept into his face. He snorted, trying to cover it, then turned to the deer behind him, as if she'd just asked him a question. "Sister wants to know what you're always reading and scribbling."

I looked at the deer. Her ears twitched. Our combined attentions confused her, but otherwise her pink head seemed as empty as a gourd.

"I read and write stories mostly," I said.

"We like stories, don't we?" he said, looking back at the deer and then at me. He leaned toward me a little. "She's not much for writing," he whispered to me. "Doesn't know how."

"Maybe she's hungry?" I ventured. "I brought sandwiches and fruit."

The boy turned to inquire. Her pink nose twitched. "She could eat."

I stood slowly to get the bag of sandwiches Harlan had set inside the trailer door, and slid the grocery bag toward the boy. He opened it, took out two sandwiches and two apples, and slid the bag back to me. He sliced the apples for Sister with his knife and fed her the slices one by one before he took one bite himself. "Thanks," he said.

"You're welcome," I told him. "And I thank you. Both of you."

"For what?"

This time, I looked right at him when I spoke. "For keeping a sharp eye on things."

He snorted and looked down at his hands and blushed a little under all that dirt.

"Would you like a story now?" I asked.

The boy looked at the deer, then turned to me and smiled. "So happens we would."

While he ate both sandwiches, I told them the story of the Japanese boy who drew cats, or what I could remember. The wild boy ate, then whittled while he listened. He especially seemed to like the part where the priest tells the boy that one day he'll be a great artist.

I pointed at the wood in the boy's hands and said, "You're an artist like the boy in the story."

He snorted again, shook his head as if this was nonsense,

his carvings nothing, but I thought he was pleased.

I was heading for the end of the story, where the Japanese boy hides in the cabinet from the evil goblin rat, when all of a sudden the wild boy stopped whittling, turned toward Henry's, and froze to listen. A few seconds later I heard Harlan tromping up the path and mumbling some dissatisfaction to himself.

I'd never seen anything move so swiftly and silently as that boy and his deer. Calm and attentive one second, they rose, turned, and disappeared into the trees in the next three, all grace and speed, like spirits or smoke or birds on the wing. I heard a few leaves rustling, but only Harlan after that.

And I hadn't even asked the boy's name or thought to warn him about the price on his head.

The stranger stepped away from his car and spat.

The cat regarded him from the porch, recognized him as the one who'd come the summer before, ahead of the girl. As before, the stranger turned in a circle, surveying the place, taking in everything as if it belonged to him by right. He sized up the chimney, the roof, the porch, even the tires on the man's truck, estimating, measuring, comparing. Then he turned to the field and regarded the man's makings with a sneer.

The cat watched anxiously as the stranger came toward the porch. He caught sight of the cat, took a lurching step forward, and stomped on the ground. And the cat shot off the porch, across the field, into the trees, the stranger's hateful laughter loud behind him.

16

I went home by way of Henry's studio, thinking about the boy and torn if I should tell Henry I'd seen him or not. It seemed like my journal and I had brought trouble to him and Sister, and something told me he didn't have a lot to fall back on. The more I thought about telling Henry, the more I worried he'd call Sheriff Bean. The sheriff would have to do his job. Hargrove and his cousin would lie like before to save their own skins, and it would be their word against the boy's. I knew who would win that fight.

But the more powerful picture that rose in my mind was Henry charging down that bank toward me on Thanksgiving Day and the way he'd stood in the line of fire. I knew he wouldn't always stand with me on everything—I had some wild hairs sometimes. But remembering us in Curtis's sights, I thought maybe he'd listen to my side and help me figure things out.

The idea of trusting Henry felt strange, though, like weakness; or risky, like leaving open a door I'd always locked. I stepped into Henry's workshop. He was welding a sculpture for Lillian's show on New Year's Eve, so wrapped up in it that he didn't hear me come in. He bent intently over it, wearing his full costume—welding jacket, apron, and hood—and sparks poured from his welding torch like it was a magic wand.

While I waited for him to notice me, I grabbed a pair of goggles off a nail and studied the new piece. Almost exactly my height and made out of shiny silver metal, it really caught and reflected the light. The bottom half was two pieces of pipe that looked like legs, like a person running full tilt, one leg straightish and forward, and the other bent at the knee behind. The upper part looked like a torso with arms flung open wide, and on top was an upturned face with coppery hair streaming out behind. Just looking at it lifted my spirits. I'd never seen Henry make anything this free or joyful before, and I was sad that he'd be sending it to New York.

I thought of the assignment Ms. Avery had given me to do over the coming Christmas break. She'd handed me a new journal and asked me what I thought of Henry's sculptures.

"I enjoyed your report," she said, "but you didn't say if you *liked* his sculptures or not."

"They're okay," I told her.

"But they don't *speak* to you?" she said, like I was missing something, some silent and important communication.

I was honest. "Not really," I said.

I liked Henry's drawings well enough, especially the ones of his dead wife. I understood that a lot of time, thought, and energy went into his sculptures. Henry was a good workman. But no, the sculptures didn't speak to me. That's when Ms. Avery said that I was to study all the sculptures Henry was making for his show and find one piece that reached deep down inside me, tugged at my heart, or spoke my name. This was the one, I thought, admiring the life in it and beginning to understand what Ms. Avery meant about looking until I really *saw*.

I stood there for almost an hour watching Henry weld and waiting for him to notice me so we could talk. I even called his name a couple of times, but his welder drowned me out, and he was wrapped up in his work. Our talk would have to wait. This time, I was ready for him, but he wasn't ready for me.

I left him to his work and took my unsettled mind around the side of the house to check the crawlspace for Mr. C. But as I did, I heard someone out front barking Henry's name, and then Fred marching out on the front porch to snap at whoever was shouting in the drive.

"Can I help you?" he said.

"My business is with Henry," a voice answered. A hateful voice I knew.

"I handle Dr. Royster's affairs," Fred said.

"It's personal business," the man said. "About the girl."

A chill rushed over me like ice-cold water. I froze in place. Ray.

"I think you'd better go," Fred said.

"I just got here," Ray insisted. "And if waiting's involved, I'll wait inside. You run tell Henry and the girl Ray Sikes is here."

"I know who you are." Fred's voice was sharp as a razor.

"Is that a fact?" Ray snarled.

"It is," said Fred. "And I don't like what I know. I think you best go, before I call the sheriff."

"Suit yourself," Ray told him. "But I got something I think'll interest them both."

"I doubt that."

"You don't know who you're talking to. I raised that girl."

"Near as I can figure, that girl raised herself," Fred said. "You don't have any rights here. Not one. You'd best move on."

My heart swelled when he said that.

"You're mistaken about me having no rights," Ray said.

"I don't think so."

"Well, I'm not going anywhere till I speak to her or Henry."

I heard Henry's workshop door slide open and saw him roll an empty welding tank outside. Fred heard it too, and shouted Henry's name good and loud.

"Everything all right?" Henry called.

"You best come," Fred called back.

Henry walked down the drive on the far side of the house. "Fred," he said, "this is the man I paid for information about Zoë."

"I thought as much," Fred said.

"You wouldn't know squat without me," Ray said nervously. "Way I see it, I've been real useful."

"Call Garland," Henry told Fred.

Fred went inside.

"Well, now," Ray said. "Just you and me again."

"Are you here for a reason?" Henry asked irritably. "I have work to do."

"Aren't you special?" Ray sneered. "Mr. Big-Shot Artist."

I couldn't stand any more. I rushed headlong around the side of the house, breathing fire. "Don't give him anything, Uncle Henry," I shouted as I ran. "He's a low-down dirty dog."

Henry lunged to grab me around the waist with one strong arm. He lifted me off the ground and held me tight.

"Turn me loose," I said, trying to wriggle free. "I'm not scared of that snake."

"That ain't kind, little girl," Ray scolded in his oily voice. "If it weren't for Uncle Ray, you wouldn't have this fine home. Why, I bet you never want for anything ever again. And who've you got to thank for that? Uncle Ray, that's who, who asks so little for his trouble."

"What do you want now?" I demanded.

"It's cold out here," Ray said, stamping his feet and looking toward the house. "I could use something warm to drink."

"In your dreams, Ray," I said. "Go."

"That ain't nice."

"I don't have nice left for you, Ray. I gave you all the nice I had. You and Mama sucked it right outta me."

"Listen to you," Ray spat. "Miss High and Mighty. You got yourself a fancy life thanks to me, and it's turned you into an uppity, snot-nosed brat."

"That's enough," Henry said.

A siren sounded, and the sheriff's car sped up the drive, lights flashing. Fred came back out on the porch as the sheriff got out of his car, shaking his head. "Mrs. Bean says I should just move in here."

"Thanks for coming," Henry told him. He set me down and loosened his hold a little.

"Good thing I was in the neighborhood," the sheriff said.

"I'm glad you're here, too, Sheriff," Ray said. "I was thinking these three might be about to draw my blood. I only wanted to offer some things I have from Zoë's mama. A whole boxful of the dear departed's possessions. Things the child might want."

"You said you took everything to the dump," I said hotly.

"Well, I did. Most everything. But I held some back, some few precious things."

"What things?" I said. "Show what you got."

Ray looked at the sheriff, whose hand was resting on his gun holster, and pointed to his own front pocket. The sheriff nodded to say it was all right, and Ray drew out a square photograph and handed it to me.

It was a black-and-white picture of a woman with a baby, but you could only see the back of her head and the baby's forehead resting on her shoulder. I couldn't tell if it was Mama and me or not.

"There's more where that came from," Ray said.

"You can't see her face or the baby's either," I said. "Could be anybody."

"It's her, all right," said Ray.

"So give what else you got and get on," I told him.

"Now, hold on, not so fast," Ray said. "This is complicated. Might be these things have come to mean something to me. Maybe a lot and I'd be hard-pressed to part with them. Fact is, I'm pretty sure I can't part with them. Leastways, not easy. They have a special place right here." He rested his open palm on his chest like he was pledging allegiance.

"How much this time?" Henry said.

Ray looked pleased. "Well, now."

"Well, what?" Henry said. "How much?"

"I hadn't decided on a figure. I was leaving that to your generous nature."

"And if I pay," Henry said, "this is the last time we'll ever see you again? The last time, the sheriff, Fred, and Zoë as my witnesses? There will be no further contact? No attempt at contact? No surprise visits, no further boxes full of mementos and photographs, no further emotional blackmail?"

"Those are hard words," Ray said.

Henry was as silent as stone.

"They sound pretty accurate to me," the sheriff put in.

"The way I see it, I'm performing a family service," Ray said. "It's hard to know if that service would be required in future. Things happen, turn up. Why, on the news just last night, I saw how documents turned up saying a little girl's dead mama had wanted her to live with somebody different, different from the blood relative she was living with, and how there'd been a settlement to compensate the disappointed party. A sizable settlement."

Ray fixed me with his ice-cold stare. My stomach turned. I felt every muscle in Henry's body tighten, and his hold tightened on me.

"What are you saying?" Henry said.

"Speak clearly," suggested the sheriff.

"I'm not saying anything," Ray told him. "Except that the future's uncertain."

"Don't pay him a dime, Uncle Henry," I said. "Whatever he's got, I don't want it. I'm finished with it, with him, with her, the whole selfish lot."

Henry looked at me. "Honestly?" he said. "You're certain?"

Ray sensed he was losing a sale. "Ain't nothing bad in the box. It's pictures and things. Trinkets. Things women save. Things you might like."

"Things I've got no use for," I said, throwing the photograph in the dirt.

I wriggled free of Henry and walked straight inside, slamming the door behind me. I leaned back against it, breathed out.

"Guess that's that," the sheriff said to Ray. "Guess you'll be leaving straight away and I won't be seeing you around here again. I'll overlook that expired license plate and inspection sticker for the next fifteen minutes, about the time it'll take you to get to the nearest county line."

Henry, Fred, and the sheriff kept silent after that. I peeked through the window. Ray looked from one stony face to the other. Then he went to the trunk of his car, shoved the key in the lock, opened the trunk, and took out a cardboard box. He carried the box five or six paces and set it on the ground.

"Tell her Merry Christmas," he spat, got in his car, and slithered down the drive.

I let Ray's box sit in the driveway all afternoon. Mr. C'mere went over and sniffed it, but he sneezed right off, which I took as a bad sign.

I sat in the front room trying to turn my thoughts back to

the boy and the deer, but that box kept claiming my attention, like it had a life of its own. One minute I thought sending it into outer space wouldn't get it far enough away from me, but the next minute my curiosity would rise till I could barely stand to sit. The *zzzsstt zzzsstt zzzsstt* of Henry's welder sounded out in the studio. Fred had gone to give Bessie her medicine and Harlan was helping the Padre, so I was alone.

I started creeping myself out, worrying that the sheriff hadn't followed Ray all the way to the county line. I worried that Ray might double back to kidnap me and hold me for ransom or claim custody of me with phony papers. Ray could still knock the joy right out of me, he and that box of Mama's things, if they really *were* her things. Anything to do with Mama could still do that to me, come out of nowhere, push my buttons, even from the grave.

Worst of all, it brought back that Saturday I was down at the library reading, away from her and Ray and all their carrying on. They'd been fighting all morning; then Ray stormed out of the house and she screamed after him, "I'm going to do it this time, you see if I don't!" I hadn't cared to spend all day listening to her snapping and whining about Ray and how hateful he was, so I headed to the library and stayed as late as I could. But when I got home an ambulance was wailing down the street, police cars were everywhere, and Ray was yelling and fuming that it was all my fault, like Mama was dead because of me.

When Henry came in, I was remembering so hard I didn't even hear him.

"You all right?" he said, and I nearly jumped out of my skin. He was leaning against the doorjamb.

I didn't answer. He sat down next to me, put his feet on the coffee table, and waited. He followed my stare out the front window to the box.

"I was having a good day. A *really* good day," I said. "Now, I'm about as low as a body can be."

"Ray has that effect on people," Henry said, like he knew exactly. "I was out in the studio feeling the same way. Anything I can do?"

I shook my head. "Ray's coming brought everything back."

"Everything is a lot," Henry said gently.

"Yeah, and it bugs me that it bugs me, you know?"

"I do."

I sighed big. We both stared some more at the box.

"I hate it that it's out there," I said. "But I hate it more that another part of me wants to know what's in it."

"Yeah, I know," Henry said, still staring at it. "But it's infected with Ray and your mama's craziness, with everything, right?"

I looked at Henry. He *knew*.

Just then Mr. C flew off the front porch and into the yard and jumped right on top of that box.

Henry and I looked at him and then at each other. Henry took my hand. "C'mon," he said.

Turned out, wasn't much in that box at all. Nothing but a bunch of old musty nightgowns and bathrobes, scarves, and junk jewelry. Not one single item I could for absolute certain identify as Mama's.

The scarecrow was Henry's idea, but I latched onto it right away. Less than an hour later, he'd welded together a metal frame for a body with a round gear for a head. Like a life-size stick figure except that the arms stretched out straight in front from the shoulders. At the ends of the arms Henry welded two horseshoes—my idea—ends up, so the luck wouldn't run out. They looked like two hands saying stop. A metal pole made a neck, spine, and lower body, which Henry stood in a stand he made from a hollow pipe welded to a round base.

He wheeled the welded frame into the front yard, and I dressed it in all eight or nine of the nightgowns and robes, draping the filmy pink, purple, blue, and green material so the skirts and sleeves would flutter in the breeze. I hung the jewelry from the horseshoes for the crows to take for their nests, then wound the head part all around with the scarves, leaving the ends long to trail behind like hair.

When I was satisfied, Henry wheeled our creation to the end of the yard next to the drive, where people would see it as they drove up. He called Fred and Bessie, and then the Padre, asking if he might come baptize it with holy water. The three of them arrived in high spirits with Harlan in tow and the Padre in his baptizing vestments. We all gathered around it as the Padre flung holy water and oil from two flasks, saying, "Out with the old and in with the new!" and everyone hooted and clapped.

And it was beautiful, more beautiful than anything that had ever come from Mama.

Harlan tipped his head from side to side, like he was trying to figure it out. "So what would you call this exactly?" he asked Henry.

"You'll have to ask the artist," Henry said, looking at me. Everybody was looking at me.

I thought for a long minute. "This is a one-of-a-kind, one-hundred-percent-guaranteed combination universal craziness deflector luck magnet and wild thing."

Henry smiled. "Otherwise known as a work of art."

17

Soon after Ray took off and Henry and I made our wild thing, the boy came back.

That afternoon Fred put up a Christmas tree in the front room, hung three stockings Bessie had quilted for Henry, me, and Mr. C'mere from the mantel, and fixed a fragrant cedar wreath to the front door. The effect was nice. I liked the piney scent of the tree and the way the little white lights encircling it twinkled in the dark at the end of the day.

Henry was working late, finishing up the last of the pieces for Lillian's New Year's show. He told me to go ahead and eat supper without him, that he'd look in on me when he came in. I saw to Mr. C on the porch, fixed myself a meat-loaf sandwich, read for a while in front of the fire, and then went upstairs to bed.

When I opened my eyes, the boy was sitting cross-legged on the rug beside my bed. He looked right at home, whittling away on a little piece of wood, letting the shavings drop to the floor. Henry's welder was still going strong out back. I wasn't afraid at all, not even startled really. I was glad to see him and realized that I'd expected him to come.

His canvas sack lay on the floor beside him. The letters *WIL* were scrawled in capitals on the bottom, facing me.

"Is that you?" I asked, pointing at the letters, and he nodded slightly. He reached in the sack and grasped something inside, then held his closed fist out to me, smiling. I reached out and he dropped an object into my open hand. It was another carving of Sister, running full out, her legs extended front and back, lifelike and graceful in every detail.

"Sister wants you to have that," Wil said. He smiled again. That he was pleased to see me showed in his face, relaxed and even handsome under all that dirt.

"I thank her. It's beautiful," I told him. "Where is she?"

He tilted his head toward the window.

"Have you had any more trouble?" I asked.

Wil snickered. "Sister's always trouble."

"I mean real trouble."

He didn't answer. "Finish the story," was all he said.

I'd forgotten I hadn't told the end of the Japanese boy's story that day at the cabin before Harlan interrupted. I wondered if Wil had come to see me or just to hear how the story came out.

"There's something you've got to know first," I said, and told him what I'd forgotten to last time, about the mayor and the reward.

He shrugged. "Think he'd let me collect it on myself?" he said in a teasing voice, though for a moment he looked uneasy.

I couldn't think of anything more to say that didn't sound

old-womanish, as Bessie said. I took the little book from my bedside table drawer where I'd left it. "There are pictures," I told him, and his eyes widened.

He slid eagerly forward but stayed on the floor. It had rained that morning, and he was damp and streaked all over with muck and red clay and leaf litter. His smell was strong, but I liked it: fresh-turned earth and wet leaves and pine sap all rolled into one.

I read the story from the beginning by the light of the full moon. I didn't want to switch on the lamp for fear Henry might see Wil through the windows when he quit and walked up the back drive. Wil leaned in close and drank up every word. He lingered a long time over each of the color illustrations, running his fingers over the parts he especially liked.

I was about two-thirds through when Henry's studio flood-lights suddenly went dark. Wil and I turned to the sound of the sliding metal doors rolling closed and Henry's footsteps on the gravel drive. When Henry paused for a few seconds, I thought maybe he'd seen us from below. But he started toward the house again and stopped to speak softly to Mr. C'mere on the porch before he came inside.

"It's just Henry," I whispered casually, hoping Wil wouldn't mind and might show himself. For the first time, the prospect of holding out on Henry didn't feel right or good. Not right or good at all.

Wil tried hard to hide it, but alarm shuddered through him. As Henry climbed the stairs, Wil looked anxiously from one side of the room to the other like a trapped animal looking for a place to dive. I pointed to the closet across from the bed, and Wil shouldered his bag and slipped silently inside. Not two seconds later, Henry stood in my door.

"I heard your voice," he said.

"I was reading out loud," I told him, holding up the book.

"In the dark?" he asked.

"Bright moon tonight."

He glanced out the window and nodded. I saw him notice the shavings on the rug, but if they struck him as odd he didn't say. There were advantages to living with a grimy man. He smiled at the book, and before I could speak he took it from my hands. He was still in his work clothes and covered with greasy dirt, he and Wil alike in their way. He switched on the lamp and sat on the floor exactly where Wil had been. I wondered if the rug was still warm. Part of me hoped Wil could keep still and quiet while Henry read, though another part wished he might give himself away.

"A long, long time ago," Henry began in his deep voice, a good one for storytelling, *"in a small country-village in Japan, there lived a poor farmer and his wife, who were very good people. They had a number of children. But the youngest child, a little boy, did not seem to be fit for hard work. He was very clever,—cleverer than all his brothers and sisters; but he was quite weak and small, and people said he could never grow very big. So his parents thought it would be better for him to become a priest than to become a farmer. They took him with them to the village-temple one day, and asked the good old priest who lived there, if he would have their little boy for his acolyte, and teach him all that a priest ought to know.*

"The boy learned quickly what the old priest taught him, and was very obedient in most things. But he had one fault. He liked to draw cats during study-hours, and to draw cats even where cats ought not to have been drawn at all.

"Whenever he found himself alone, he drew cats. He drew them on the margins of the priest's books, and on all the screens of the temple, and on the walls, and on the pillars. Several times the priest told him this was not right; but he did not stop drawing cats. He drew them because he could not really help it. He had what is called 'the genius of an artist,' and just for that reason he was not quite fit to be an acolyte.

"One day after he had drawn some very clever pictures of cats upon a paper screen, the old priest said to him severely—'My boy, you must go away from this temple at once. You will never make a good priest, but perhaps you will become a great artist. Now let me give you a last piece of advice, and be sure you never forget it. Avoid large places at night;—keep to small!'"

I saw a flash of movement behind the closet keyhole and heard stirring that made my stomach lurch. The space under the closet door darkened. Wil was pressing himself up against the door. It seemed odd to me how a boy who could keep himself so silent in the woods had so little talent for it indoors.

I held my breath, waiting to see if Henry had heard, but he was focused on the story and kept right on reading, telling how the Japanese boy traveled to a second temple, one possessed by an evil goblin rat. He read how the boy went inside to find the priest and, finding none, found ink and empty screens and began to paint cats, a great many cats, cat after cat after cat for hours and hours, until, feeling sleepy, the boy remembered the old priest's words and crawled inside a small cabinet to sleep.

I heard Wil grasp the handle of the closet door and saw it turn a little as Henry told how the boy woke to a screaming commotion in the night, heard the sounds of a desperate fight to the death just outside the little cabinet door; how the terrified boy stayed in his cabinet until morning, when he crawled out and saw an enormous goblin rat, "bigger than a cow," lying dead and bloody on the temple floor.

"But who or what could have killed it?" Henry read, his baritone rising and full of deep feeling. *"There was no man or other creature to be seen. Suddenly the boy observed that the mouths of all the cats he had drawn the night before, were red and wet with blood. Then he knew that the goblin had been killed by the cats which he had drawn. And then also, for the first time, he understood why the wise old priest had said to him:—'Avoid large places at night;—keep to small!'*

"Afterward that boy became a very famous artist. Some of the cats which he drew are still shown to travellers in Japan."

Henry closed the book and gazed fondly at its cover, then handed it back to me. He stood and kissed me on the forehead, and as he did, I had the hopeful and anxious notion that Wil might spring out from behind the closet door and ask for another story. But Wil kept silent and the door stayed closed. Henry said good night and headed for the stairs.

"Oh, I almost forgot," he said, turning back. "I saw the white deer, just now, when I was coming in from the studio. She was standing at the edge of the wood, like she was waiting for someone. She ran off when she saw me."

"Did she seem all right?" I asked, suddenly wondering if

he'd known Wil was here all along, if this had been some kind of test, a test I'd failed miserably.

"Fine," he said, no hint of any motive in his voice. "Magical."

"Thanks for the story, Uncle Henry."

"Good night, Zo'," he said, and went downstairs.

I heard him slide his supper out of the oven, switch off the kitchen lights, and come back up the stairs. Wil stayed put. I turned over like I was sleeping as Henry padded by my room and headed up to his own. I waited till I heard his work clothes hit the floor and water running in his tub. When I felt sure he wouldn't hear, I crept out of bed, put my ear to the door, and whispered Wil's name, but he didn't answer. "Wil," I whispered again, but no answer came.

I opened the door slowly. Wil lay sound asleep in his own small place, curled up on his side between my red boots and my sneakers, his head resting on his sack. He looked like a kid of five or six. I set the little book on the floor beside him and took the extra blanket off my bed to cover him. He didn't stir. I left the door open, but just a crack. I hoped he'd stay for the night where it was safe, and wake me—and Henry too—before he left again.

I only wish he had.

The cat couldn't sleep. After the boy stole into the house and up the stairs, he worried. And when the boy crept out again and he and the deer raced off together into the woods, the cat kept thinking he heard strange noises coming from the trees.

It was bitterly cold, even on the porch. The water was frozen in his bowl and the stars glistened overhead like bits of ice. He stared through the window in the small door the man's helper had made beside the big one. He looked up the hillside of steps the girl was always climbing or coming down. He knew she was up there. It was beyond him what could be worth such effort, but something was, something that took her away from him every night. He wished she would come down to him now.

Lately she spent more

and more time with her ever-multiplying kind. Traitor girl. Didn't she see the boy for the trouble he was? Smell it? The cat's anxiety grew. He tapped the little door with his paw. Nothing. He tapped it again. It swung open a little. He gave it a good swat. It swung in, then out, then closed. He pushed it open with his nose and sniffed the warm, girl-scented air, then drew back, afraid. Stupid door. He curled up in front of it, tried to sleep.

Not long after, as if she'd heard him, the girl crept down the stairs. The big door opened and she slipped outside, bundled in clothes and wrapped in a thick blanket. He looked up at her, meowed.

She spoke to him sweetly, bent down, put out her hand. He lost all caution. He sniffed it, licked her fingers, let her softly scratch his head, under his chin, down his back.

She caressed him, rubbed his belly and ears, whispered to him softly, then curled up warm against him. They lay awake together for a long time, watching the wood's edge, listening.

At dawn she got up and walked to the trees, seemed to search for something, then returned to him, shivering and shaking her head. She went inside, propped open the little door, and lay down on the floor at the foot of the stairs. From there she called to him over and over in her high, soft voice, and after a while he couldn't bear it and went in to her. She laughed as he hugged the walls, kept one wary eye on the little open door, and bolted through it like a shot when the man came sleepily down the stairs.

He let me touch him, Uncle Henry! she cried. I just had to be patient, is all. Till he saw he could trust me.

The man smiled a little, as though she had said something important, and gently rubbed the top of her head.

After the man went to his workshop, the girl stayed in the hall. She left the little door propped open, understood that an exit should always be open to him. The cat went in, then out, all day. Outside, he missed her attentions and the house, warm and dry. Her sweet voice coaxed him back inside. Inside, he missed fresh air, the vault of sky, the leafy sponge of earth beneath his feet. In and out he went, back and forth, trying to decide.

That evening, she spread a cloth on the floor of a farther front room and called again for him to come. At first he balked, sat stubbornly in the hall near his door, staring at her. She lay on the floor of the room and stared right back, more stubborn than he was, waiting. He went to her, finally, felt the heat of the fire. How the crackling warmth caressed him! He rolled before it, bathed himself in heat, and slept.

Later, unsatisfied still, she climbed the stairs, left a morsel of meat on each step. She stood at the top, far above, calling him. He stared up at her. She called and called, but he did not budge.

She gave up late, frowned and turned her back on him, went wherever she went up there. He ducked out his door. He slept fitfully on the porch, near the earth, the trees, the life he knew. He dreamed of shut doors and stairs, steps that went up and up as far as he could see, stairs he climbed until his short legs ached and his heart was close to bursting, until just after sunup when the shrill ringing woke him, woke the whole sleeping world.

18

The phone woke us before daybreak.

Upstairs, Henry groaned and cursed and took his ex-wife's name in vain. But the second he answered it his tone completely changed. It wasn't Susan calling.

"Fred," I heard him say. "Calm down, Fred. Calm down and make sense." Then: "What do you mean she's gone? Gone where?" And finally, after a long, listening silence, he said, "Certainly a stroke could explain it. A lot of things could."

Half a minute later he took the steps two at the time down to my room. I was sitting up in bed when he came. "What's happened to Bessie?" I said.

Fred hadn't been calm enough to make perfect sense. From what Henry could gather, Bessie had wandered off sometime in the night. She'd left the front door open and a meandering note about seeing the cabin and the white deer, saying she had to lay eyes on them, tell the wild boy something before she died.

"Fred and the sheriff want our help," he said. "You and Maud know those woods better than anyone."

"Course I'll help," I said, jumping out of bed, pulling on my jeans, boots, and sweater faster than I've ever moved in my life. Henry went upstairs to finish dressing and I heard him on the phone with Harlan. The phone rang again and I heard him say, "Any news, Garland?" so I knew it was the sheriff. Then I heard him dial and say, "Maud, Henry Royster, sorry to wake you at this early hour."

But I knew right off who was best suited to find Bessie.

I slid down the banister and threw on my coat, plus an extra in case I found her without one. I snatched the flashlight off the kitchen counter and sped out the door. I heard Henry hollering for me to wait, but I kept running. I raced through the woods to the cabin, thankful for the moonlight, calling Wil's name as I went, yelling, "Wil, where are you? I need your help!" But I got all the way to the trailer without seeing anybody or hearing one human or animal sound.

The night was still and cold, not a leaf stirring. Both the trailer and cabin were pitch-dark and empty, looking like lonely, abandoned places. The only thing I heard was my own sharp breathing.

I started screaming Bessie's name as loud as I could in every direction, my breath leaving me in clouds. I hollered till I was hoarse, half expecting Wil to appear any minute out of the darkness with Bessie in tow. But there was no one. Nothing. Even the wind was still.

Maud arrived first, calling out ahead so I'd know. A second later Henry stormed up the path with his doctor bag, griping that I'd left without him and taken the only flashlight in the house, sending him to the studio to find another. The sheriff and his deputy came right after that, the sheriff grumbling how we all had serious acreage to cover between the cabin and Fred's. "If she *is* between here and Fred's," he added, "and hasn't gotten turned around or heading in a whole other direction." He said the Padre and others were calling around for volunteers to help us look, but he wasn't sure when they'd get here. Fred and Harlan were working their way here from Fred and Bessie's place. The sheriff barked out directional assignments to those present.

The once-silent woods grew noisy with twigs snapping, leaves rustling, and Bessie's name shouted in every octave. Flashlight beams sliced the darkness. Henry and I headed farther north. I tried to split off alone so Wil might find me, but Henry refused to leave my side. At first it irritated me. Wil wouldn't show himself with Henry near, and we'd never find Bessie without Wil's help. But as Henry and I tramped along together in the deep light, stumbling over the same roots and snagging our clothes on the same branches, each calling to the other to watch out for this low limb or that rotted log, I was glad to have Henry beside me. I mean, what did I think I was going to do if Wil wasn't around when I found Bessie and she was bad off and couldn't walk? Just what could one scrawny kid do?

Dawn haloed the tree line when Henry and I stopped a minute in the gray light to listen and get our bearings. He scanned the woods in all directions, squinting hard at anything that might be Bessie's crumpled shape. The land here was rocky, and from a distance the big, lichen-covered boulders looked almost human.

"What do you think Bessie meant, saying she wanted to see

the cabin before she died?" I asked him, barely able to speak that last word.

He hesitated.

"The truth," I said.

"The truth," he said, and heaved a big sigh, "is that Bessie's lived far longer than anybody thought she would."

"Because of you."

"No," he said, shaking his head. His gray eyes met mine. "I'm not being modest. Bessie's hung on beyond all reason for a very long time. Her heart keeps going beyond medical understanding."

We tramped along in gloomy silence after that. I thought about Mama dying and how hard it had been to lose somebody I *didn't* love. I wasn't ready to lose the first person I did.

Suddenly the sheriff yelled Henry's name back of us, saying his deputy'd gashed his head. Henry told me to wait there and took off toward the sheriff's voice at a trot. The distance grew between us until Henry disappeared and I was finally alone.

A few seconds later, I heard excited voices from the opposite direction. Thinking it might be Fred and Harlan or some of the other searchers, I headed for the sound. The voices were coming from the far side of some large boulders, but when I got close, I stopped, recognizing one voice's ugly sound. Quiet as I could, I crept to the rocks, found holds for climbing up, and shimmied on my stomach to peer over the top.

I nearly cried out at the scene below me. Hargrove and his daddy, the mayor, stood in a big clearing about fifty feet from Sister, who was tied by her neck to a tree at the clearing's edge.

Without Wil to calm her, she was out of her mind with fear, but the harder she yanked to get free, the more the rope rubbed her neck bloody and raw. I scanned the trees for Wil, trying to see where he was, knowing he had to be the one who'd tied her there and wondering what idiot idea made him leave her that way.

Hargrove stood right below me, turned toward the pale roped creature struggling before him. I couldn't see his expression, but beside him, his daddy, a shotgun by his side, beamed with pride, reminding me of Ray and the pleasure he'd taken in killing animals.

"I don't have a *white* deer on my trophy wall," he was telling Hargrove. "Wouldn't she be perfect?"

"But Daddy, she's—" Hargrove said.

"She's *what?*" his daddy interrupted. "Don't be soft, Hargrove. You're too much like your mother that way. In fact, *you* take her," his father said, handing his shotgun to Hargrove. "It's time you took your first prize."

Hargrove accepted the gun, and his daddy backed away.

"Well?" his father said. "Hurry up."

"But she's so beautiful," Hargrove told him.

"Of course she's beautiful," his daddy said, as if that was obvious and Hargrove not very bright. "That's the point. If you take her, she'll be beautiful forever on the wall of my den. And you'll be able to say, 'I did that.'"

"Look what I found," a voice called from the far side of the clearing. Curtis, the hunter from Thanksgiving, appeared, holding up Wil's bow and arrows in one hand and nudging someone forward with the other. Wil staggered before him into dim light. I wondered why Wil seemed so unsteady, and then saw he was carrying something heavy stretched across both his arms. The weight of his load kept him planted, though he twitched in horror at the sight of Sister and the gun in Hargrove's hands. I was about to shout to Wil when I made out what he was carrying. It was Bessie—Bessie, limp and still as death.

"I'm claiming that reward!" Curtis shouted.

"Hurry up and take your shot," the mayor told Hargrove. "Then I'll call the sheriff on my cell phone and say you've found Mrs. Montgomery *and* the boy who shot you. You'll be the hero of the day."

Hargrove squirmed and shifted from one foot to the other, not at all sharing his father's rush. I remembered the afternoon behind the school when I'd seen Hargrove scratch Sparky's belly and rub behind his ears. Hargrove looked from Sister to his daddy to Wil, from Wil to his daddy and back to Sister. Sister, though still bug-eyed with fear, had stopped thrashing since Wil had come into the clearing. My heart grew sick and near bursting with rage at the thought of what would happen next.

Hargrove surprised me then. He leaned the shotgun against the boulders behind him and walked slowly over to Sister, talking to her sweet and low, trying to reassure her. She stood quivering, wary and breathing quick, watching to see what he would do. He walked a wide circle around her and slipped a folding knife from his front pocket. Glaring hard at his daddy, he sawed through the rope at the tree and cut Sister free.

She stood for a moment, not sure of her freedom, but when the mayor lunged for the shotgun, she bolted into the woods.

I wish I could say I thought about what I did next, but I didn't. As I stood up on top of that rock, Wil and Hargrove caught sight of me, amazement and horror on their faces. Curtis saw Wil glance up, and as Curtis looked up too, I shrieked and threw myself off that boulder right on top of the mayor as he turned to aim at Sister. I hit hard, felt a sharp pain, and heard the shotgun go off with an earsplitting blast just as Henry hollered, "Zoë! No!"—the last words I heard for a good while.

19

Bessie lay in the hospital bed not seeming at all like herself without her headscarf and quilts, looking more like a wrinkled child. I'd never seen her without a scarf. What hair she had was silver and close-cropped like a man's. Tubes ran from the inside of her elbow and her right side to plastic bags hanging on metal stands. Her skin was as gray as rain, and her nose and mouth were covered with a mask connected to a tank beside the bed. I had to keep reminding myself it was Bessie.

A machine next to the bed gave off a steady *beep, beep, beep,* and I watched the raggedy rhythm of her heart on the little screen and found it reassuring. It meant I didn't have to watch the shallow rise and fall of her chest to make sure she was still breathing. I focused all my energies on giving the Padre's Lord God Almighty, reportedly in Heaven, a piece of my agitated mind. Maybe we all had to die sometime, I told Him, but please not Bessie, and not at Christmas, not after everything else that had happened. If He took her now, He could take His stingy, stonehearted love and shove it for all time. A kid can only take so much.

Fred was off having a conference with Henry and the other doctors about Bessie. She was out of the woods for now, but Dr. Miller, who had set my broken arm, said we'd have to wait a while to be sure she'd stay that way. I liked Dr. Miller. She listened to me like I was a grown-up.

"You're Dr. Royster's daughter?" she asked while she wrapped my arm.

"Niece," I told her.

"There's certainly a resemblance. I don't know what we'd do without his help every week at the free clinic."

She told me Bessie would surely have died if Wil hadn't found her when he did. "All of you got her here just in time," she said. "Your friend Wil is a hero."

Bessie shifted under the covers, and her eyes opened, bright as ever. "Baby, what are you doing here?" she asked, real soft.

I could hardly hear her through the little mask. I leaned in closer.

"Henry said to come get him if you woke up. Want me to?"

She shook her head. "Not just yet. Remind me how I got here so I don't sound like an old fool."

I told her what I knew. How after she'd got it in her mind to take a midnight walk, Wil had found her in the woods and tried to carry her to get help. How Hargrove had stood up to his daddy, and how I'd had to jump off some boulders onto the mayor's head. The mayor was okay, more or less, I said, but I wouldn't want to be Hargrove after what had happened with his daddy.

"I wish I'd been awake when everything happened," Bessie whispered.

"Don't worry," I told her, "I'm putting it all in my memoir."

"I want somebody pretty to play me in the movie," she said. "Where's the boy now?"

"Gone. Nobody knows where. He ran off after his deer in all the confusion."

"Good for them." She caught sight of the cast on my left arm.

"I broke it when I jumped. It doesn't hurt much, though." I paused, wanting to say something else.

"Spit it out," she said.

"Henry said you nearly died."

She softly patted the mattress between us. "Come up here."

I climbed carefully over the rail and lay on my side facing her, my back against the gate.

"You know what I'm going to remember most about today?" she said.

I shook my head.

"What I'm going to remember is the best day I've had in a long time."

I thought it was a strange thing to say.

"The absolute best day," she went on. "I busted out of my jail cell and actually walked beyond my own backyard, *far* beyond it! That may not sound like much to you, but honey, I was living! When I walked into those woods, the first thing I thought was how long I'd let Fred and everybody worry over my poor heart so much that it had about stopped beating. Not today."

"But you didn't make it to the cabin."

"But I tried, didn't I? I threw off my chains and tried. *You* taught me to do that. Taught me not to let anything or anybody keep me from doing what my spirit was made to do."

She smiled a weak smile. When she turned her face full my way, I saw that the left side was stiffer than the right. Her eyes closed just a little. "From now on, nobody's keeping me from doing what that spirit moves me to do. And right now, it's moving me to lie here next to you and take a little nap."

She fell asleep almost at once. I lay in the bed thinking about what she'd said. I thought about Henry, and the hard time Fred and the sheriff had given him about letting me do what I needed to do. I'd ignored him, disobeyed him outright, scared him half to death, kept the truth from him, and brought a stray cat, a wild boy, people with guns, and two of Mama's loser friends into his life. Not that I thought I could've done any different. And still he'd left the reins loose and the barn door open.

I drifted off to sleep for a while, and when I woke, Henry was standing at the side of the bed, frowning over Bessie's chart. He was wearing his surgeon clothes and was as clean as I'd ever seen him.

He looked so grim and serious that for a minute I was sure he was still furious with me. But when he saw I was awake, he set the chart on the bedside table, leaned over the side rail, and lifted me in his strong arms. He hugged me hard to him, the way you hold somebody when you feared you'd lose them and didn't. I lay my head against his chest and breathed in his faint grease, turpentine, and metal-dust smell, the Henry smell that no amount of scrubbing ever washed away, the smell I was beginning to love.

Fred stayed with Bessie at the hospital that night, and Henry and I rode home to get some sleep. It was nearly five in the morning when we got there. Henry went straight up to bed. Before I headed to my room, I fed and rubbed Mr. C'mere, who was waiting for me on the porch. I scanned the woods' edge for Wil, both hoping he'd come and hoping he wouldn't.

The mayor had upped his reward for Wil's capture to ten thousand dollars. Sheriff Bean told the mayor that he'd better prepare to explain his decision to bring a shotgun to search for Bessie, a gun that had *gone off* and might have killed any one of the searchers nearby. The mayor countered that the gun had been for protection from delinquents with bows and arrows and that the gun's firing had been *my* fault—claims, the sheriff said, he'd let the district attorney wrestle with. The sheriff doubted that the mayor's allegations would stick if Wil was found. He *had* saved Bessie's life, and winging Hargrove, who was drunk and trespassing, had been his first offense. But because Wil was a nobody migrant boy, he wouldn't have options or a moment's peace with everybody trying to catch him and cash in. If he was caught, the sheriff thought, he'd likely be sent to a state home. His best hope was to move on, disappear.

My heart was heavy thinking about Wil and Bessie as I climbed the stairs, but what I found when I switched on my light about made me shout with joy. I stood in my doorway and stared. The whole room—the floor, the window seat, the dresser, the bedside table, the bookcase—was covered with Wil's prized possessions: birds' nests and eggs, beautiful rocks, a turtle shell, pinecones, animal bones, lichen-covered twigs, and dozens of feathers in every color of bird.

On my bedside table was Wil's cigar box, the one I'd found in the cabin when I was first there, and Wil lay fast asleep in my bed.

He woke and smiled a little as I came in, but I saw how exhausted he was. I shut the door so Henry wouldn't hear us, switched off the light, and lay down facing him on the bed.

He ran his fingers over the cast on my arm. "That was a dumb thing to do," he said, looking pleased I'd done it.

"You should talk," I said. "They're all looking for you. Two-thirds of them want to give us medals and the other third want to lock us up. How's Sister?"

"Safe for now. That lady was right."

"What lady?"

"The one I found. She said I should put Sister somewhere safe and get as far away from here as I could. Gave me two hundred dollars. Said the mayor's a dog with a bone. That sooner or later he'll see Sister dead and me in jail."

"Where will you go? You got family?"

He shook his head. "I'll move with the pickers, like always. It's no big thing."

I could tell that last part was a huge lie, that his heart was hurting at the very thought. "Well, it's a big thing to me."

Wil smiled.

"Won't you let the sheriff, Fred, and Uncle Henry see if they can help you?" I asked. "Finding Bessie made you a hero to most. Won't you let them try?"

"Dog with a bone," he repeated. "That lady's smart."

I looked into his weary eyes. Deep down, I knew he and Bessie were right. "Will you write and let me know where you are?" I asked him.

"Don't read or write."

"Well, you better *learn*," I told him and he grinned.

I reached for his hand then, and he let me take it. We lay together quietly after that for the half-minute it took us to fall asleep.

Wil was gone when Henry woke me the next morning, like I knew he would be.

He'd left every one of his treasures, though, exactly as they had been the night before. They were even more beautiful with the sun streaming in like honey through my windows. Henry took them in, not at all surprised by the news of Wil's visit— though I didn't let on he'd stayed the whole night.

I took the cigar box off my night table and lifted the lid. Inside, in a bed of dry leaves, were the six carved animals: otter and squirrel, possum and mouse, raccoon and deer. I showed them to Henry one by one, and then showed him the carving of Mr. C'mere and the second one of Sister. Henry turned each one in the light and marveled, saying how lifelike they were and how gifted Wil was. Underneath them, the face of the boy's mama peered up at me, the photograph I'd seen the first day at the cabin. I handed it to Henry and read him the single word scrawled on the back. "That's Wil's mama," I said. "I'm pretty sure she's dead."

Henry nodded sadly and handed the picture back to me.

I started to set it and the little animals back in the box, but caught sight of something else in the bottom under the leaves, a second photograph that wasn't there before. I brushed it off and held it to the light so Henry and I could look at it together. It was a wedding picture, but a sorry one, made sorrier by the bent corners and creases, like Wil had carried it in his pocket. The bride was the same woman as in the first photograph, Wil's mama. Her dress and veil weren't white or new, though they looked clean and pressed. This time, though, she seemed happy with the man she loved beside her, and she smiled into a skimpy bouquet of wilted roadside flowers.

The man was different. His face was turned away like he was looking over his shoulder to see what fearsome thing was gaining on him. You couldn't see but the far right side of his face, just a cheek, the tail of an eyebrow, a sideburn, a misshapen ear. His suit swallowed him and seemed old-timey, like the thrift-store specials Mama's friends used to buy. The woman's left hand was reaching for her husband's, but he stood on tiptoe, leaning away from her, looking hollow and light, like a man-sized balloon about to take flight. One look would have told any sensible person that this fella wasn't a stayer, that the first thing he'd do on arriving anywhere was look for the exits. I'd had half a dozen or more stepdaddies exactly like him.

I handed the picture to Henry, who turned it over to see if anything was written on the back. His eyes widened at what he read. He leaned in close to show me what it said.

For the longest time the best thing about never knowing my daddy was that I could picture him how I liked. I could imagine he was funny, handsome, or kind. I could dream he was the sort of man who found his little girl in a dark wood and carried her home. I could kid myself that only something real important kept him from tucking me in at night or tending me when I was sick, and that he lost sleep over the thought of all he was missing by being away from me. Stupid, I know, but all evidence to the contrary, I'd dreamed it just the same. Till now.

I read the spidery handwriting four times before the meaning sank in, and twice more after that to be sure—though what it said made perfect sense when I thought about it. I looked up at Henry, who flipped the picture back to the front side to know for the first time the face of his brother, Owen, while I gazed for the first time on my real daddy and the daddy of my brother, Wil, who was this minute following in our father's footsteps, taking flight. Henry put his arm around my shoulder and pulled me close. I wrapped mine around him and did the same.

Mr. and Mrs. Owen Royster, read the woman's delicate handwriting, *on ther weddin day.*

The boy left the house before dawn. He and the cat regarded each other—the boy standing for a time on the porch, so that the cat noticed, for the first time, how much he resembled the man.

The boy did not hurry. There was some-thing lonesome and adrift about him, and the cat followed as he climbed the path to the cabin. There, the boy walked to the dogwood where his mother was buried and stood for a while. After that, he rolled the two-wheeled machine off the cabin porch and poured an acrid-smelling liquid into its stomach. He climbed on its back and brought it briefly to sputtering life, then silenced it. He pushed it quietly through the woods, back to the man's house. He glanced up at the girl's window, turned to nod at the cat, and then pushed the machine down the dark drive.

The boy's leaving unsettled the cat, disquieted the very trees. The girl wouldn't be up for hours. The cat headed off beyond the stone garden to the steepled house to hunt rats.

When he got there, a terrible racket resounded from the building's insides. Bright light streamed from the high windows into the near

yard. Behind them, heavy objects
crashed to the floor, glass and pottery shattered,
metal rattled and clanged. Whatever was trapped inside bounded
from one end of the building to the other, one minute thrashing in
front, the next galloping to the back, the next climbing high, toward
the steeple, as if it were learning to fly.

At dawn, a truck drove up. The man's helper guided the old man
with the cane to the building's arched front doors. They unlocked the
doors and opened them. The white deer bounded out, wild-eyed,
knocking both men on their rears, and vaulted into the far trees.

20

Henry's New Year's Eve opening in New York was a big success, even by Lillian's standards. Lillian was put out that there were only "fourteen legitimate Roysters," as she put it, Henry and I having included our *Crazy Deflector Wild Thing* at the last minute; but when it sold *first,* she shut up and took the check. When Henry said that the money was mine to add to my rubber-banded bankroll, I nearly died. After deducting Lillian's piggy fifty percent, I still got *four thousand five hundred dollars*—or will, when Lillian gets around to forking it over.

"Congratulations," Henry said. "You've sold your first work of art."

By the end of the night, nearly every sculpture had sold and everybody was saying how it was Henry's best work ever. Henry behaved himself, mostly, except when Lillian told him that one of her best clients wanted to buy one of the big pieces, but only if Henry would paint it hot pink. I smiled to hear Henry hollering across the crowded room, "If she wants it pink, she can buy a flipping can of Rust-Oleum and paint it herself."

I thought: *That's my uncle Henry.*

I hated to admit it, but it was a good party. Those snooty people's rich and famous brains were swimming in high-dollar alcohol, the extra expense not making them one bit brighter than any other drunk. Half the women flirted with Henry, but I didn't blame them. When the band churned up around eleven to play something we could move to, Henry scooped me up and set me on the bar and we danced along it and back, people laughing and moving out of the way and cheering us on. I told Henry he moved pretty well for an old man, and he said I shook it all right for a girl with no hips. Franklin cut in then and Henry danced with Helen, who had hips aplenty. Knowing Bessie was in the hospital back home didn't let any of us take anything too seriously.

I'd read to her from my journals every day over Christmas and after, right up until the day we left. She liked hearing about herself, especially the part where Wil rescued her and I hurled myself onto the mayor's head. We'd spent nearly every minute of Christmas in her hospital room. She was coming along slowly and had trouble remembering things, and Fred said my reading to her from my journal was about the only thing that cheered her. I read her favorite parts to her over and over, and every time she'd laugh like she was hearing them for the first time, which maybe she was. That's what friends are for, she told me, to remember all the things you've forgotten. Fred called right before the gallery opening to say she could hardly wait to hear what happened at the end. He said Harlan was busy cleaning up the church after Wil had shut Sister inside. Wil must've been thinking of the Japanese boy hiding in the temple when he put her there. That was the last anybody had seen of him or the deer.

Just before midnight, Henry and I escaped the party to sit on Lillian's gallery roof. Henry drank champagne right out of the bottle while I sipped hot cocoa. We were twenty stories up in the freezing cold with easily ten or twelve zillion lights above and below us, sparkling and winking in all directions. I was on top of the world.

I huddled up to Henry and thought of the beautiful sculpture he'd given me for Christmas—the one that had spoken to me that day in his studio—saying it was for all the holidays and birthdays he'd missed. He called it *Wild Thing*, set it right in the front yard. Fred said it looked just like me and announced that, come spring, he was planting a flowerbed around it, with bleeding heart, love-in-a-mist, and heartsease.

I smiled, thinking about the laptop computer Franklin and Helen had sent me to write on. I'd also found a beautiful quilt under the tree from Bessie with the wonders of my new life stitched into the nine pieced squares: Mr. C'mere, Henry's farmhouse, a log cabin, the Padre with a crooked halo, Fred's red truck, Sister and Wil running through the trees, a pack of Juicy Fruit for Sheriff Bean, an embroidered representation of my journal with *Zoë's Memoir* stitched on the cover, and a red and silver sequined heart with wings. For his present, I'd shown Henry the dedication page of my memoir on my computer screen. *To Henry*, it said, *with love*. First time I'd ever written that to anyone.

A chain of firecrackers went off somewhere, yanking me

back to the present, and all of a sudden hooting and shouting and horns blowing down below us signaled the start of the New Year, making me officially twelve.

Henry jumped up and gave me a twirl, saying "Happy New Year" and then singing "Happy Birthday," and as the New York night whirled by I thought about all that had happened in the last year—things happy and sad, mean and kind, terrible and wonderful, things beginning and ending, all in some measure all the time. I'd been trying all day to think of the word to describe that everything-all-at-once feeling, the one I'd had nearly all my life, the way I felt when I thought about Mama, or looked at my half-brother's carved animals or the picture of his mama and our daddy, the feeling I saw in Henry's face when he was remembering his dead wife or in Fred's when he was worrying over Bessie, or in Hargrove's when he set Sister free.

Bittersweet, it seemed to me.

Right as I was thinking that, Franklin came up behind us and whispered into Henry's ear.

The crunch of gravel woke him as the long black car crawled up the snowy drive.

For several days, strangers had come to fill his bowls. Missing the girl, he slept lightly, one ear cocked, curled up at the base of the shiny new object in the yard.

The object was unmistakably the girl. An oval of delicate silver outlined her face, traced truly the shape of her wide eyes, sat atop her graceful neck. Fine strands of coppery hair blew back from her face. The metal sketched her arms, torso, legs. She seemed as light as air, running headlong, her arms flung back, fierce with life, and at the center of her chest spun a silver heart with two tiny outstretched wings, each cupped to whirl the heart in the slightest breeze. And bounding beside her, in sinuous silver, the cat.

The day the man set it there, the girl careened out of the house. The man stood smiling, letting her dance around it, open her gift before he twirled her in his arms. Soon after, they drove off together, and in the lonesome days since, silence had been the music of the day. Snow had fallen, spread its white blanket over the woods and trees. The place grew quiet as death.

Now a squat man got out of the car and buttoned his coat against the cold. He walked to the door and knocked, stomped the snow from his shoes. He peered in through the glass, shaded his eyes with one hand, then walked to the steps to survey the snowy yard. Seeing no one, he walked back to the man's workshop. The cat jumped on the hood of the car and looked through the glass inside. Instead of a long box, a large, lidded pot sat on the front seat.

Hello, kitty, the squat man said, coming back up the path. Guess they're still at the church. Terrible to be late to your own funeral, but we're all behind, what with the snow.

Cars began pulling into the drive. The old woman who'd stuck the cat's behind with a needle got out and walked around to help the old man with the cane.

The man drove up then, his helper in the seat beside him, and the cat's heart leapt to see the girl jump out and run to him. He let her scoop him up, legs in the air. She kissed him between the eyes, then set him gently in the drive. Seen Sister? she asked the old woman.

The old woman nodded. Every day. Likes the salt lick I got her. Any word from your brother?

The girl shook her head.

The man went around to his helper's door. His helper looked shrunken, crumpled as a dry leaf. The small group gathered around him as a car with flashing lights drove up. More got out, front and back. Everyone talked and embraced. The man and the girl spoke together, deciding things.

Shall we then? the man said.

They walked in slow, silent procession across the snowy field. The sky was overcast, considering the gray matters of clouds, whether to snow or rain. A sudden wind spun the whirling parts of the man's makings. A few whined or creaked as they turned, like singing. The man walked beside his helper, who hugged the covered pot. The others followed, two by two, the cat and the girl last.

They crowded inside the stone garden, circling a small, perfect square dug deep. The helper set the pot tenderly into the hole. The girl opened the book she was always scribbling in, took a long breath, and spoke softly for a time, pausing to wipe her wet cheeks, turn a page. All of their faces grew wet then, and the cat glanced up at the gray sky. And it began to snow.

21

Bessie's service was beautiful—the Padre's church full of fresh flowers even in winter—and afterward those I loved came to the house for the burial. A miraculously goodly number, a number that had been zero only a few months before. Only Bessie herself and Wil were missing.

I had to hand it to my brother: when he wanted to disappear, he vanished like a dream in daylight. There wasn't one single sign of him anywhere. Despite local and state law enforcement searching the highways and byways and the greedy citizenry combing the small towns and wild places in between to collect the mayor's hateful bounty, Wil kept out of sight.

Helen and Franklin flew in from New York and Sheriff and Mrs. Bean got back from Christmas with their daughters just in time for the service at the church. Maud actually wore a dress. We all sat with Fred and Fred's cousin Henrietta in the front rows reserved for family. Every pew was filled—a huge turnout for someone who'd hardly left her house in years.

Bessie had given Fred and the Padre strict instructions about how her service should go, threatening to come back and haunt them if they didn't do as she said. Unlike the solemn services I'd attended with Manny's mother, Bessie's had joyful music and laughter. The Padre spread one of her quilts over the altar. He said how God had walked again on this earth in the person of Bessie Parsons Montgomery, as surely as Christ had walked here two thousand years before. Heads nodded. *Amen*, those present said, and God seemed a hair friendlier to me then, if only a hair.

I stood on a communion wine crate at the lectern and read the parts Bessie liked best from my memoir, though it was all I could do to read without crying. I read the part where she said folks were starved for beauty. I read how she'd refused a heart transplant, saying she wouldn't be herself with someone else's heart beating inside her. And I read the Thanksgiving entry, where Bessie had spoken the truth about little Garland Bean's rescue and laid the local lie bare.

People stood and clapped when I was done. I knew they were clapping for Bessie.

I read from more recent parts of my journal at the burial—about Henry's New York opening and Sister's brush with religion in the Padre's pews—because Bessie hadn't lived to enjoy them. I liked to think she could hear. Henry had her grave dug next to Mama's, just like she'd asked. Bessie thought that she and Mama might have things to say to each other, if such conversations were possible. That they might become friends.

The snow started again right after the burial, and for a while everyone looked a little lost and kept to themselves. Fred lingered at the graveyard with Bessie. He couldn't get it out of his head that she'd be lonely there all by herself. When he finally came up to the house, he headed mechanically for the kitchen and stood staring at the cabinets, the refrigerator, and the stove like he was standing on the moon.

Maud led him to a chair. After that he stayed quiet, the way anybody'd be when his whole reason for living had been yanked away. He hardly seemed to hear when people spoke to him. Henry kept close by him, and though I didn't hear them exchange twenty words, I understood whole conversations taking place in the silence between them.

The Padre sat by the front room fire sipping sherry. By the second glass he'd declared Bessie beatified and by the third glass sainted. To my eyes, his collar didn't afford him any more protection against loss than the next person. He looked plain and simple, like a man who'd just buried his best friend.

Harlan paced and muttered to himself about Wil's taking the motorcycle, sure something bad would happen because he hadn't had a chance to check the air in the new tires or replace the old brakes.

Then people started to come, some who'd been at the church and some who hadn't, though no invitations had been issued, no formal reception planned. "People know," Helen said. "It was like that after my mother died. They just come."

And come they did, in snow-dusted dribs and drabs all the rest of the day: farmers who knew Fred and who had brought Henry their plows to weld, people who'd bought Fred's flowers and whose hearts Henry had mended, people who'd known what Bessie had meant to one or all of us. They filled the kitchen with casseroles and the house with happy memories of Bessie and speculation about Wil.

Near day's end Ms. Avery came, saying there was somebody outside who was too shy to come in. I put on my coat and went out. At first I didn't see anything but falling snow, but then I saw Hargrove, hunkered down next to Mr. C'mere under the sculpture Henry had made for me.

I walked out toward them. "Hey, Hargrove," I said.

"Hey." He stood up, hands in his pockets.

"That was a good thing you did for Sister," I told him.

He nodded but stared at his feet. "How is she?"

"Fine. Ms. Booker's looking after her. Is your daddy mad?"

He looked off toward the end of drive. "Mad doesn't describe it." He went quiet for a few seconds, then mumbled, "He's sending me away."

"What!"

"To school."

"Oh."

He pulled a small brown sack out of his coat pocket and handed it to me. He turned away as I took off the paper. My red journal. "Sorry I took it," he said. "Sorry about the cabin, too. Wasn't me who tore it up, but I don't guess that matters."

"It matters," I told him, and then we just stood there together watching it snow.

I remembered what Harlan had said to me about Mama, the good her dying had done me. Maybe being sent off to school would be the best thing that could happen to Hargrove. Maybe getting away from his daddy would give the art- and animal-loving boy inside him a chance of coming to light. Like me getting away from Mama. But I didn't know Hargrove well enough to say that out loud.

"You're a good drawer," I said instead. "You ought to keep doing it."

For the first time he looked at me.

"You want to come inside?" I asked.

He shook his head. "Okay if I stay out here and look around?"

"Sure it is."

"See ya," he said, waving a little, wandering off toward the sculptures in the side yard.

"Don't be a stranger," I said back.

He and Ms. Avery left a little while after that, and soon the others left too, and it was just Henry and me, Fred, Maud, Franklin and Helen. We sat by the fire wondering about Wil. I brought down his little carvings from my room, and we passed them carefully from hand to hand as if they were holy objects. Everyone marveled at Wil's exquisite work, Henry most of all. He said how grand it was to have another artist in the family and wondered if Wil had any notion how really good they were, far better than anything he'd done at Wil's age. Maud got quiet then, saying Wil made her think about my daddy, Owen, and whether she'd done right by him, giving him up.

I listened some while they talked, but I felt far, far away. I was mourning Wil's loss as much as Bessie's, maybe more. Though Wil wasn't dead, I felt cheated of him.

I tried to convince myself that he wasn't gone for good. I

knew what the north woods meant to him. Since the morning Wil left, I'd walked up to the cabin every day I could, sure I'd find another little carving waiting for me, warm ashes in the fireplace, the bed slept in, any sign he was still around, though I found none. Sometimes I'd think I had glimpsed him in the trees because of a flash of white, a boyish trick of the light, but a second later I'd know otherwise.

I wondered if he'd be a picker for the rest of his life. Move from backwater to backwater. Never learn to read or write. Never know who or what he was. Not that there was anything wrong with picking soybeans or strawberries. But I couldn't help but wonder what, if given the knowledge and the chance, he might do with his life. Never knowing—to me, that was the worst loss of all.

I must have been tired, because that was the last thing I thought before I fell asleep. One minute I was sitting with everybody in front of the fire, and the next thing I was waking up to find my head in Henry's lap and Henry drawing on my cast, sketching a picture of Mr. C.

"Is everybody gone?" I said.

Henry nodded. "The snow's getting deep. It's just the three of us now," he said, nodding at the far edge of the hearth rug where Mr. C'mere lay fast asleep.

"Hey, buddy," I said, and his tail swished.

Then suddenly it hit me. It must've been Henry's drawing of Mr. C that did it. I sat bolt upright, wide awake. I got up like I'd been shot out of a cannon, sending poor Mr. C bolting out his little door. I raced up the stairs to my room.

"Are you all right?" Henry called from the foot of the stairs.

"I got to see something," I hollered back, and started searching. I was a human tornado. I jerked open drawers, pulled the sheets and covers off my bed, the pillows off the window seat, the books off the bookshelves, trying to remember the last time I'd seen it. If it was still here, it was somewhere in this room. If it was gone, there was only one reason.

I searched every inch of the closet and shimmied under the bed with the dust bunnies, Henry all the while calling from the bottom of the stairs, "Zoë! What's wrong? What in God's name!"

"I'm looking for something!" I shouted.

"Do you want me to help you find it?"

"I don't want to find it!"

"What on earth?"

"Never mind!"

I looked everywhere in that room, not finding it anywhere. I knew it was the one thing Wil had taken with him, though he'd left everything else—his whole life—behind him.

I took the banister, sliding straight into Henry's arms. "He took the book! He took the book!"

"Who are you talking about?" Henry said. "What book?"

"*Wil,*" I said, as though it was as obvious as red paint on a barn. "The book about the Japanese boy. The one who drew cats. It's the *one* thing he took. A book he can't even *read.*"

"I don't understand."

"Don't you see, Uncle Henry?" I blurted, smiling. "He *knows.*"

"Knows?"

"He knows he's one of us."

Henry stopped looking at me like I was touched in the head. He saw at once what I was saying. He smiled and nodded and carried me back into the front room, where we restoked the fire, and where Mr. C—persuaded by the deepening snow and a plate of Maud's tuna casserole—soon rejoined us. And I told them the story of the boy who listened at closet doors. The boy who'd lived by his own uncommon lights. The boy who loved wild things. Stories I suspected they already knew.

ACKNOWLEDGMENTS

This story first strayed into my life on four white pink-padded paws.

A big, wild, mustachioed black-and-white cat lumbered into my yard and heart more than two decades ago and became my shadow and soul mate for ten extraordinary years. He and I were pals like Lassie and Timmy or Rascal and Sterling North. Our years together included a genuine miracle, and maybe I'll get to write that story one day. Until then, I hope this book begins to thank Mr. C'mere for all he gave me.

My sculptor-husband, Mike Roig, was my muse, reader, goad, fierce defender, and boon companion during this book's journey. I thank him for making me persevere and stand up for my story with Zoë's ferocity and toughness, and for filling the house with love and flowers on discouraging days.

I thank other first readers Luli Gray, Peter Guzzardi, Jane Harwell, Vicki Smith, and Frances Wood, and copy editor Katarina Rice.

My final thanks go to my editor, Joy Neaves, who shepherded, nurtured, and encouraged this book for nearly five years. Joy, Helen Robinson, and Nancy Hogan, thank you for the work and heart you put into making *Wild Things* beautiful and possible.

—*Clay Carmichael*

QUESTIONS FOR MORE THOUGHT ABOUT THE STORY

Some readers tell me they wish to think, talk, and/or journal more deeply about the characters and subjects in Wild Things. *I offer the questions below as a starting point. Some are from readers, teachers, or librarians; others are questions I've wondered on or continue to wonder about myself. Feel free to add and wonder on questions of your own.* —Clay Carmichael

Why do you think the book is called *Wild Things*?

What does wildness mean to each of the characters in the book? To you? Is wildness a good thing, and if so, in what ways? Can wildness be dangerous, harmful, or lonely? Is tameness better? Why or why not? Can too much tameness hurt people and animals too?

What role does anger have in the book? We usually think of anger as a negative emotion. Do Zoë's anger and fierceness help her in some ways? Is fierceness sometimes necessary? When? Does anger hurt Zoë and Henry in some ways? How? How have anger or fierceness hurt or helped you? Have you ever had to stand up for something you believed in? What happened?

Zoë and the wild cat have lived hard lives. They find it hard to trust, because no one so far has earned their trust. Is learning to trust important for them? Is trusting important or necessary to you? Has a wild or stray animal ever learned to trust you or someone you know?

When do you think Zoë starts to trust Henry? Why does she decide to trust him at that moment? Does her new trust affect anything that happens afterwards? Have you ever trusted someone who then betrayed you? Have you ever distrusted someone and later changed your mind?

At one point, Zoë thinks, *"The minute you talked about something, you risked losing it"* (p. 113). What does this statement mean to you?

Helen, Henry's artist-friend from New York, says her spirit would die if she couldn't paint (p. 145). What in your life is so important to you that your spirit would die if you couldn't do it? Is there something you feel you were born to do? What is it that you're most passionate about?

Henry stands between the hunter and the white deer to protect Zoë (pp. 155–156). Who in your life would you choose to stand up for in the face of danger? Why did you choose this individual?

On Thanksgiving, Bessie convinces the group gathered at Henry's house to take in Harlan. Do you think she was right to do this? Have you ever had to persuade a person or group to do a good deed for someone else? What happened?

Does Zoë see Harlan the same way at the end of the story as she saw him at the beginning? Have you ever given anyone a second chance? Has anyone ever given you a second chance?

Henry and Zoë both had mothers with similar problems. How else are Henry and Zoë alike? How are they different? If you had to say where they might be and what they might be doing four or five years after the story ends, where do you think they'd be living and what would they be doing?

In Chapter 16, Zoë and Henry make a sculpture together using Zoë's mother's old things. Zoë calls it *"a one-of-a-kind, one-hundred-percent-guaranteed combination universal craziness deflector luck magnet and wild thing,"* to which Henry adds, *"Otherwise known as a work of art"* (p. 197). How does art help the characters in the book, especially Henry and Zoë? Do you think art helped Henry when he was Zoë's age? Do you think Zoë might become a writer or an artist like Henry?

What do you think happens to Wil after the story ends? Do you think he'll ever see Zoë and Henry again? If no, why not? If yes, how do you think this will happen? What might they say to each other?

What about Hargrove? At the end of the book he shows an obvious interest in Henry's sculpture. Do you think he might become an artist one day? Why or why not? Why do you think he starts off angry at Zoë?

What do you think would be Zoë's definition of a family? What is yours? Do families have to be blood-related to each other? Is there a family you are born into and another family you can make for yourself? Do families have to be composed of people, or can animals be part of families too?

Zoë says that animals' love is purer than people's (p. 22). What does she mean by this? Do you think that's true? Have you ever experienced this purer love yourself?

"Miss Avery said that I was to study all the sculptures Henry was making for his show and find one piece that reached deep down inside me, tugged at my heart, or spoke my name" (pp. 187–188). The names of many well-known artists—most sculptors like Henry—are listed at the bottom of page 34. How many of them do you recognize? Pick two or three of these artists, choosing at least one you don't know, and look up their work in the library or on the Internet. Does any of the artwork tug at your heart or speak your name? Might looking at or living with art change the way you think about or look at things? How?

For more information about Clay Carmichael and *Wild Things*, visit claycarmichael.com.